T

IN THE

HEAD

A Ricky Burns Mystery

C. K. LAURENCE

JERRY LYONS

For information:
cklaurence@gmail.com

ISBN
9798390179550

Front cover art by
Zachary Laurence

Published in conjunction with
Ronni Sanlo Literary
www.ronnisanlo.com

Printed in the United States of America

TWO

IN THE

HEAD

A Ricky Burns Mystery

C. K. LAURENCE

JERRY LYONS

OTHER WORKS BY C. K. LAURENCE

THE QUARTERBACK'S DEMONS

THE MYSTERY OF JESSICA BENSON

DEDICATION

C.K. Laurence thanks everyone who was so supportive and helpful throughout the process of writing this mystery. Special kudos and love to my baby brother Jay Kirschner, Esq., his incredible assistant Colette Boyer, and my dear friend Karen Raben, M.D. Also, a shout out to my husband for putting up with me, and my kids, Josh, Abigail, Emily and Zachary and their kids (who I am crazy about) Evan, Cameron, Samantha, Zoe and Maya.

Jerry Lyons thanks First Grade Detectives John Clinton and Vinnie Carrera, two great detectives who taught me how to be a good one. I also want to thank my former boss and still friend Detective Sergeant Tom Burke for allowing John Cornicello, Mike Sapraicone, Jeff Aiello and me leeway to do the job the way it should be done. And of course, my wife Sharon, my children Stephanie, Jerry III, Jessica, Mary, Erin and stepdaughter Stephanie for putting up with me while I lived the life that enabled me to write this story. Finally, I'd like to thank attorneys Jose Baez, Lisabeth Fryer, Mike Kessler and Jay Kirschner for allowing me to work on some of the most exciting cases in America.

CHAPTER ONE

*R*icky Burns' twenty years as a New York City Homicide Detective were coming to an end. He was conflicted about his retirement, after all at forty-two he didn't feel ready to give up the job he loved. As a cop, Ricky survived two shootouts and was the first guy the Department went to on the tough, grittier cases. He was smart and had been lucky to stay alive. His former partner was shot and crippled in one of the shootouts, and another detective on his team was dead and gone. When his eleven year-old son came to him, tears welled up in his eyes, and said, "Dad, what if you don't win the next one?", smart money told Ricky to take his pension and get the hell out of Dodge. So whether he was ready or not, he put in his papers and prepared to start Chapter Two of his life.

CHAPTER TWO

It wasn't easy for Ricky to clean out his desk and walk out of Major Case for the last time. The handsome detective spent more than twenty years of his life policing, and despite his son's encouragement to leave while he could get out whole, abandoning his work bothered him more than he expected. He was still young enough to begin a new career, but the only thing he really loved was solving cases and making a difference. He decided to get his license and become a private investigator.

Sitting alone in his small apartment, he agonized over what was next for him. That's when he got the phone call that changed everything.

It had always been a dream of his to live on a houseboat. Every time he passed the 79th Street Boat Basin over the years, he'd thought about it. Jake Sloan, an old buddy of his, moved to Florida ten years prior. He'd invited Ricky to visit so many times, but he had no interest in Florida and he'd never taken advantage of the offers. Now Jake, who knew Ricky had retired, was on the phone with a proposition. He owned a houseboat on Indian Creek in Miami Beach. Because it sat empty, it had been burglarized twice. He wanted Ricky to come live on the houseboat. He wasn't asking for rent; he only wanted Ricky to be there to keep an eye on it. As long as Ricky lived there, he'd never pay rent. Ricky said he'd give it some thought.

CHAPTER THREE

*T*wo ex-wives with hands out for monthly alimony and child support meant Ricky had little time to decide where to go and what to do. His pension was half of what his salary was and that just wasn't going to cut it. He figured he didn't have to live in New York to do private investigations, and with his reputation he hoped to have all the work he could handle. That houseboat surely sounded good though. Living on a houseboat was a long-time dream of his, and rent-free was tempting. The more he thought about it, the better it sounded. They were expecting a bitter winter in New York, so "What the hell," he said out loud. "I'm moving south."

CHAPTER FOUR

*G*etting out of his lease was easy. He was the last tenant in a formerly rent controlled apartment building. It was renovated to attract tenants who were more interested in prestige than price. They were even adding a doorman. The new building owner had been encouraging Ricky to move for a year now. He'd made Ricky more offers than he could count. Ricky had no intention of leaving—especially now that the building was remodeled and safe. The manager could barely contain his enthusiasm when Ricky told him he was leaving at the end of the month.

It was the first time in his life he was making a move he hadn't been planning. He had never been much for school, so when he graduated high school, he joined the Navy. It was there, working underwater demolitions, he decided he wanted to be a cop. He went to the Police Academy as soon as he was discharged from the service. Initially he walked a beat in uniform, but it didn't take long for word of his outstanding work to get to headquarters. He was fast-tracked to Detective and assigned to the Robbery Squad. From Robbery he quickly moved to Major Crimes/Homicide, which he loved either despite the danger or because of it. Had it not been for his son's tears, he'd still be out there chasing bad guys on the streets of New York.

His decision was made though, and now, hoping his reputation would help him get work to earn the money he needed, he was on his way to sunny Miami Beach and a houseboat he'd never seen.

CHAPTER FIVE

After a month of packing, donating and trashing what he wasn't taking, Ricky took to the road. Interstate 95 all the way. The houseboat was furnished so all he had to take was clothes and stuff he couldn't part with yet. Everything he had was in his car. He hoped his son was happy but he was feeling terribly conflicted. He'd never been a spur of the moment type of guy, and this new life was taking him far away from his children and his comfort zone. Jake was his only friend in Miami, and now he would be his landlord too. They had spoken several times over the month. Ricky asked Jake to keep an eye open for an inexpensive small office from which he could hang his private investigator shingle. Jake said there was no reason for an office. He could work from the houseboat and live where he worked. After thinking about it, Ricky figured he could at least start there and see where it went.

Jake, now wealthy, lived in one of the overwhelming number of sky-scraping condominiums on the ocean. He was relieved that his old friend was going to be on the boat. He trusted Ricky without reservation. He knew Ricky Burns was the answer to his problem. Nobody messed with Ricky!

Ricky drove straight to Jake's apartment and they rode to the boat together. Ricky thought it looked nice but not so much inside. When Jake opened the door, he had to bite back a disappointed gasp. It was badly run down, dusty and all around disappointing. His place in New York might have been small and nothing to brag about, but he'd always kept it clean and it never looked worn and old.

When he found his voice, Ricky gulped, "My, but this is really something."

Jake smiled. "Well, I know I haven't kept it up, but a little cleaning and a coat of paint and you'll be good, no? I have someone coming tomorrow to do some fixing up. I wanted to have it done by the time you got here, but have you tried to get a handyman lately?"

Just a little cleaning up? Ricky thought, but managed a smile and said, "Yeah. Good. I'm sure it will be more impressive when it's cleaned up. Did the burglars get anything worth anything?"

"Nah. Just junk which is all I left here. The boat is so exposed now. Used to be a line of houseboats here. We all looked after one another. Some were sunk and some left when Hurricane Andrew hit. Then when that guy who killed Versace hid out on one of them and did himself in when cops got close, everyone seemed to lose their taste for life on the water and left. So here we are. I first turned it into an Airbnb but renters didn't take care of shit, and I worked too hard on this baby to see it destroyed. So, for now at least, she's all yours to love."

Ricky smiled for lack of words as Jake beckoned him to follow for the full tour. Ricky followed, thinking about how much Jake had changed. He seemed more sophisticated and worldly. He guessed money did that. Living in a penthouse overlooking the turquoise Miami Beach ocean gave Jake a self-assurance he'd never had when they were young.

Once out of the living room, it was less shabby. There was a galley kitchen with all modern appliances. Ricky's bedroom was good and had a king size bed. Ricky's smile grew larger when Jake showed him the other bedroom which was set up as a fully equipped office.

"I used this as my office during the COVID shut down. Just this week I re-equipped it for you. Nice water view, bluetooth and everything you need to set up your computer and voila! You're a private eye."

Ricky finally found his voice and told Jake he loved it. Now all he needed to do was find clients. His resume spoke volumes about his value.

"Not to worry about work, Ricky. I've got you covered. I do some serious networking. I've already given your name and resume to several attorneys. Some of them even knew about your reputation in New York. You are a hero man. You're going to be, excuse the expression, 'JAKE'!"

"A hero's nothing but a sandwich, Jake. You've done more work on my future than I have. Damn. I did this so quickly, it didn't even hit me that you were the only one I knew here. No one knows me but you. It's a screwy way to go on with my life."

"Well, you will be hearing from them. You've worked cases that didn't just resonate in New York. You've gotten plenty of publicity here, too."

The two talked for a while, shared a couple of beers that Jake had stocked in the refrigerator and promised to keep in touch. Jake grabbed an Uber home and Ricky was finally alone. He looked around and made a mental note to just stay out of the living room for now, and hoped he'd be out on cases soon.

CHAPTER SIX

It was on the third day, while sitting in his office counting the floorboards that his cell phone finally rang showing an unidentified number. Not wanting to appear anxious, he waited three rings before answering.

"Ricky Burns Agency."

"Is this Mr. Burns?"

"Yes it is. How can I help you?"

"Mr. Burns, are you sure you're getting the best deal on car insurance?"

Ricky looked at his phone for a second, shook his head and told him he was and to have a good day. Then he hit the red button disconnecting him. He had savings, and of course his pension, but he didn't want to have to go into his savings unless it was an emergency. Maybe he'd been too quick to cut and run from New York.

Moments later the phone rang again and Ricky picked it up on the first ring. "I said I've got good insurance. Now lose my number."

"Oh! I'm so sorry," said a woman who seemed to have been crying. "I must have called the wrong number."

"Who were you trying to reach, m'am?"

"I was looking for the Burns Detective Agency. Really, I am so sorry to have bothered you."

"No bother. This is Ricky Burns. Sorry about the way I answered. I was dealing with a pesky salesman. You've got the right number. How can I help you?"

The woman sounded awfully choked up. Ricky had a pretty good idea why she was calling and he knew he was right when she blurted out "My daughter is gone! The police aren't doing anything and they've even insinuated I might have something to do with her disappearance. I could never hurt my daughter. She's my only child. She has, um, a disability and I'm terrified something awful has happened to her. Will you help me?"

"That's what I do. We'll need to meet as soon as possible but let me get some details now. A good place to start would be your name."

"Yes, of course. I'm sorry..."

"Ms., stop apologizing. So far as I know you haven't done anything wrong," Ricky interrupted.

"Sor… I mean, I'm Catherine Wickens. Cathy. My daughter is Meggie."

"Okay, Ms. Wickens, how old is Meggie and when did she go missing?"

"She's eighteen, and please, call me Cathy."

"Okay, Cathy. You mentioned Meggie had a disability. Do you think that might have had something to do with it?"

"I think it has everything to do with it. That and me."

"Whoa, whoa. Back up. Take a deep breath and don't start blaming yourself. In my opinion, no one ever goes missing. Somebody knows where she is and all we have to do is find that person. Please continue."

"Meggie's eighteen and exceptionally beautiful. A natural beauty. And she's sweet and kind but she trusts everyone, to a fault." She grew silent.

"Okay. I'm a little confused here, Cathy. You're saying her disability is her beauty?"

More silence from the client so Ricky went quiet as well. Ricky Burns had great instincts. More importantly, he was a bit of an empath. He could feel when to speak, when to be quiet, when to be a good guy and when to be a bad guy. He especially knew when to walk away.

Cathy gave an anguished laugh that was more like a croak. "Maybe in a way. She was brain damaged at birth. She looks like a movie star."

"I'll need to know everything as soon as possible. Are you able to come to my office?"

"I don't want to leave my house in case Meggie comes home. She has to come home. My daughter has the face and body of a woman, but her brain never passed six years old. Can you come to me?"

"Absolutely. I want you to be comfortable when we talk. I'll need pictures of Meggie. The first thing we need to do is get posters out to see if that brings any quick information. If we meet today, I can have them done at Sir Speedy by tomorrow."

CHAPTER SEVEN

Catherine Wickens' home was on Pine Tree Drive. Once upon a time, Pine Tree was known as "Millionaire Road." It happened to be right across a small bridge from the houseboat. It was one of those big, old Deco places. She was standing in the doorway when he drove up. As soon as he got out of his car, she beckoned him in.

Wickens looked to be in her early forties. Ricky could see she must have been really beautiful herself, but now she looked worn. She was blonde, but her hair just hung. Her eyes were red from crying, but there was no make-up to run. Her demeanor screamed agony.

Catherine's story wasn't one he hadn't heard before. She and her daughter walked around the block together every day. Meggie was anxious to get out that morning but Cathy got a call on the landline that she knew would tie her up for a couple of minutes. Meggie was whining and started crying so Catherine told her to go outside and wait for her. Not more than five minutes went by but when Cathy went outside, Meggie was nowhere to be found. She wasn't a fast walker but Catherine traveled the entire neighborhood calling for her with no response. Meggie always stopped to smell flowers or watch a squirrel. Cathy figured they must have crossed paths and Meggie must already be home. She was not there. The police told her she'd have to wait forty-eight hours to report it and implied she might have had something to do with the disappearance because she couldn't handle her brain damaged daughter.

Cathy gave him a number of pictures for a poster and told him she would take care of getting them hung. Ricky saw she was right about Meggie's beauty. She was exceptional. He paid extra and got the posters back to her that day then began the tedious task of interviewing everyone in the neighborhood. After covering a five block area with no one having seen Meggie, he started back to the houses where no one had been home. Finally, he got a hit. Someone a block away from Catherine's home had seen her get into a van with a guy. The woman hadn't thought anything about it because Meggie seemed to get in the car willingly. She assumed it was someone Meggie knew.

Never assume, Ricky thought. Now he had to start asking neighbors if they had surveillance videos and would they allow him to review them.

Because Ricky had an honest face that was also easy on the eyes and an easy manner, people were receptive to his requests and most everyone in the area agreed to allow him to review their video.

"There," Ricky said out loud, "I've got you!" On one of the videos he clearly saw the van, the guy and Meggie. He was even able to make out the license plate which he ran immediately. He didn't want to get Cathy's hopes up, so he said nothing to her.

As soon as he got the name, William Sampson, and his address, he headed straight to his house. He didn't live on the Beach but in Hialeah. Two different worlds.

CHAPTER EIGHT

When Ricky got to Hialeah, he parked down the block and walked to Sampson's house. Sampson's record reflected he'd had a few juvenile run-ins with the law, but the files were sealed. He patted his Glock which was neatly hidden under his jacket. The last thing he wanted was to have to use it, but if he still had that girl, Ricky would do whatever he could to get her back. Not that he wanted any gunplay. He'd been there, done that and he didn't want to go there again.

Ricky knocked loudly on the door and called out "Mr. Sampson? Ricky Burns. Can we speak for a minute."

He heard laughter from inside and "What? Your dick burns? Who the fuck are you?"

"I'm a private investigator. I just need a few minutes of your time sir."

"Yeah? Why?"

Ricky had enough. "Either open the door and give me a couple of minutes or I'm going to kick the door down." Which he promptly did.

Inside he saw Sampson going for a revolver on the dining room table. Ricky quickly drew his Glock and shouted, "Don't move!" But Sampson grabbed it anyway and pointed it toward Ricky.

"Don't do it!" Ricky warned but was ignored. Sampson aimed, and Ricky shot him. He was quick and sure but shot to wound not to kill the guy.

Sampson went down and Ricky flew toward him to grab his gun. It was a struggle but Sampson was slowed by the wound to his shoulder and Ricky prevailed.

"Where's the girl?" he practically yelled.

"I'm shot. Get an ambulance. Help me!"

"I'll take care of you when you tell me what you've done with Meggie."

"Shit man. She's in the bedroom. She was a lousy lay anyway. All she does is whine when I remove the tape. Take her after you call for help."

Ricky had no intention of calling for help before he found the girl and knew she was alive. He did, and she was, but she was naked and pretty badly beaten and her mouth was covered with masking tape. She looked frightened as Ricky came toward her. She was tied up and shaking like a leaf.

"It's okay Meggie. Your mommy sent me to get you and take you home. I won't hurt you and neither will he, ever again. He moved slowly toward her and removed the tape first, then took her into his arms and cradled her softly. "You're going to be fine. I'm going to take the ropes off and call your mommy to tell her you're safe."

"He hurt me," she cried. "He put his wee wee into my mouth and my, my…"

"I know, Meggie, I know."

The ropes were now off and he wrapped her in the sheet. He asked where her clothes were and she began to cry again.

"He threw them away."

After calling for an ambulance, Ricky told Meggie to stay in the bedroom while he went out to check on Sampson who was holding his bleeding shoulder and whining for help. Ricky gave him a towel to press against the wound, tied his hands and feet with the rope from Meggie and went back to sit with her until the ambulance arrived. Then he called Catherine to tell her to meet him at Mt. Sinai Hospital in about an hour where he'd have them check her to make sure she wasn't hurt worse than he could see. He also wanted to make sure they did a rape kit so the evidence could be preserved as well as the case against Sampson

CHAPTER NINE

Catherine Wickens was a generous woman. Ricky and she had never discussed a fee, but she gave him a five thousand dollar check. He argued it was way too much but she would have none of it. He'd saved her daughter and it was worth more than the five thousand she gave him.

It got plenty of news coverage. "Former NYC Homicide Cop Saves the Day" was the headline in the Miami Herald and all the local news shows carried the story. It made for some good publicity which he needed. The missing persons calls started coming in immediately. Ricky didn't love missing persons cases but they were jobs and he knew the more he did, the more chance his name would be heard and eventually he felt confident other cases would be coming in soon.

He'd just finished one of those missing persons cases when a call came in from a Miami attorney. He'd seen Ricky's resume and followed his work since he'd come south. Jay Kirschman, a criminal defense attorney, had actually called his old precinct in New York to inquire about him. He was as careful about choosing his investigators as he was choosing his clients. Kirschman had been a public defender for years. Back then he had to take what he got but once his reputation was made, he went into private practice and made it even bigger.

Ricky listened to what the attorney had to say, then asked, "Are you sure you checked me out well enough?"

Kirschman laughed. "Oh, sarcasm. We should work well together. I caught a murder case. It's big. When can you meet with me? My office is on Brickell Avenue."

"I'm open tomorrow. What time is good for you?"

"How about ten? It's important we get started as soon as possible."

"Ten it is. See you then." Ricky said.

Ricky was still smarting from the shoot-out with William Sampson. His son convinced him to get out of police work to avoid the chance of being killed yet he'd managed to stumble into another shoot-out on his first case. A simple missing persons case, and he'd faced his son's worst nightmare.

The rest of the cases he'd worked on were relatively civil and he'd avoided any trouble, but now, after getting the call he'd been hoping for, he was back in a funk. He ran it around in his head for the rest of the day. Should he or shouldn't he?

It just wasn't in Ricky Burns' nature to pass on a good murder case so he decided to go for it. The next morning he put on a suit and tie to meet the attorney and get started on his first homicide case since he'd left the Force.

CHAPTER TEN

Ricky arrived at Kirschman's office at ten sharp. He couldn't help but be impressed by the office. Plush carpeting, a huge picture window framing Biscayne Bay, and a very attractive assistant. She smiled as he walked in and said, "You must be Ricky Burns."

"I am," he responded, straightening his tie.

"Wow. I feel like I know you. Jay had me researching your past to be sure you were as good as he'd heard. You passed with flying colors, which isn't easy to do with my boss." Another one of those really nice smiles flashed.

"Yeah. I got that from him when he called. I'm glad I passed muster. There's nothing I like better than a good old fashioned, bloody murder case."

"Did he tell you anything about it when you spoke?"

"Just that it was a big murder case."

"Oh boy, is it! Let me tell him you're here. I'm Collette and it looks like we're going to be working together." She got up before she finished talking and walked toward a closed door, hips seductively swaying, knocked twice, opened it and disappeared.

A couple of minutes passed before she came out with Kirschman beside her, or so he guessed. The attorney reached out to Ricky, took his hand, and gripping it firmly, shook it. He was a tall, good looking guy, Ricky figured he was in his mid to late thirties. He had intense brown eyes, curly brown hair and the look of a man who knew what he was doing.

"Good to have you on board. I've only heard great stuff about you and your work."

"Yeah," Ricky grimaced. "It sounds like you and Collette know more about me than my ex-wives do."

Kirschman chuckled and Collette gave another of her great smiles. The three of them walked back to Kirschman's office which was even more impressive than the reception area. The outstanding view of the Bay was what made it. The furniture was nice, Mahogany desk, and the thick carpeting, but the teal Bay was the jewel. Four swivel chairs faced the massive desk. Kirschman took his seat at the desk and Collette motioned Ricky over to the chairs. She sat. He sat and the saga began.

CHAPTER ELEVEN

Kirschman, Ricky and Collette made small talk for a short time, but almost immediately got into the guts of the case. He hadn't lied when he said it was big.

"So," Kirschman began, "you follow football, Ricky?"

"Jets, Jets, Jets!"

"Not in here, please. This is a Miami Demons sanctuary. At least it is from now on 'til we finish this case. We will be representing the best interests of Wide Receiver Ron Ramirez."

"The Ramirez that signed a forty million dollar contract with twenty-four million dollars guaranteed up front a couple of years ago, who's now charged with murder?" Ricky was really interested now.

Collette popped in with, "*Two* Counts of Murder One and another of Attempted Murder."

Smiling, Kirschman asked, "You in, Burns?"

"Am I in? Don't you see me sitting right in front of you, Mr. Kirschman?"

"Mr. Kirschman's my dad. Call me Jay. And I'm guessing, yes. Our client will be here at one o'clock so I want to bring you up to speed for that meeting."

CHAPTER TWELVE

"*F*irst of all," Jay said, "He's out on bond. Million dollars for each murder charge was all they asked."

"Did they take away his passport?" Ricky asked.

"No, they thought he might want to use it. Of *course* they took away his passport!" Jay snapped.

"Okay. Sarcasm. We're even. Shall we continue?" Ricky was smiling.

"This will be our first real sit down with Ramirez. I met him at the jail briefly, pleaded him not guilty and told him to be here today. He's a tough guy. Swears he's not guilty regardless of what the evidence is or what they say. From what I can see, they've got a pretty good case. You're going to have your work cut out for you, Ricky."

"Good. That's how I like it, and like I tell all my ex-wives, if you have no expectations, I'll never disappoint you." Ricky smiled.

"You're going to have to come up with newer shtick, man. That's older than I am!" Jay chuckled.

They talked about the case most of the morning, broke for lunch at noon and were in Jay's office when Collette stuck her head in and told them Ramirez was there. Jay nodded and Collette ushered the 6'4" Wide Receiver into the room which he seemed to fill.

Ron Ramirez wore a tee shirt that clung to his muscular frame, jeans and sneakers. He walked in, looked at Ricky and asked "Who's he?"

"He is Ricky Burns, the investigator that's going to save your ass," Kirschman shot back at him. "Along with me," he added.

"Good to meet you, Burns. I am innocent."

Jay grimaced, and said, "All my clients are innocent. We just have to make a jury believe it."

"No man. I swear. I did not do these killings. Look, I'm a bad guy. I know that. I've done a lot of things I ain't proud of, but I did not do this."

"They've got a lot on you, Ron. How about you start from the beginning and tell us exactly what happened that night. Don't leave anything out," Kirschman said

Ramirez was silent for a couple of minutes. He looked from Jay to Ricky to Collette who had just come back in with a notepad and taken a seat next to Ricky.

"Why's she in here?" Ron looked pissed.

"She's my assistant and will be taking notes. Deal with it. She has the same attorney/client relationship as I. Anything you say stays here." Jay, looking somewhat unhappy himself, responded.

"Okay, man. Take it easy. I just want to tell you something that can't get out of this office. I wanna come clean, but I don't want it to come back and bite me in the ass."

"All three of us are here to get you out of these murder charges. No one will ever hear or read what you tell us," Jay reassured him. "I can only speak for us, though, Ron. If you have or do tell others, that's on your watch."

"You gotta believe I'm innocent when you talk about the murders, but so's you'll believe I'm not lying, I'll tell you this. I did kill a guy a while back. It was what I had to do to get into a gang. I was young and didn't believe I'd ever get out of the 'hood. I wanted my back and my family to have protection and that was the best way to get it. You people don't get it, I know, but it's a way of life."

Jay sat forward in his chair and asked, "Who'd you kill?"

"I shot James Bacon. He was a piece of shit that had been trying to move in on my posse's territory. I don't think anybody even remembers it now. It's been five years."

"There's no Statute of Limitations on murder," Ricky warned.

"Yeah, so?" Ramirez asked.

"Just make sure you realize that. Keep it to yourself, we'll keep it to ourselves and if no one else decides to out you, we'll be fine." Jay added.

"Not something I'm likely to bring up in small talk, but I wanted you to believe me when I told you I did not kill those two guys!"

Jay nodded and asked Ron to go back to the night of the murders and relate exactly what happened.

"Okay. I can do that. I picked up my buddy JoJo around eleven that night. We were going clubbing on South Beach."

"What club?" Ricky asked."

"Brick."

"Okay, go on."

"I got to feeling like I was suffocating there. Everyone seemed to recognize me. I couldn't even get a VIP Room, it was so crowded. This one wanted a picture with me. Another wanted my autograph. After a few minutes I told JoJo we should leave. I was getting hungry anyway. We couldn't have been there more than ten minutes. As soon as we got outside, the guy I took a picture with came up to me and started talking. JoJo took my keys and said he'd get the car. I stayed there but he took his damn time getting back to get me. Anyway, when he picks me up, I get into the passenger seat and he speeds off to Prime 112. JoJo's gun was on the console. I asked him what was up with that. He tells me to toss it out the window as far as I could. I didn't know what that boy was into but I didn't want no part of it so's I picked it up by the barrel and it was history. Then he tells me he had a beef with some guys who'd ripped him off in a drug deal. 'Great' I told him. Now my fucking prints are on the gun. He laughed, and said if I had thrown it far enough out there, no one would ever see either of our prints. Prime 112 was already closed when we got there so JoJo says we should go to his girl's house. She'd feed us, and she lived just over the bridge into the City. As soon as I got to Maria's house…"

Ricky interrupted, "Maria have a last name?"

"Gonzalez. Can I go on now, or you got more questions?"

"Don't get smart with me, Ramirez. I'm here to help you out of a bad jam. I need every bit of information you can give us about that night. If I ask a question, it's for a reason," Ricky was pissed.

"Yeah, I get it. Didn't mean to step on your last nerve. Anyway, first thing I did when I got to her house was go to her computer to check out the Internet and see if there was any word on JoJo's shootings. Nothing was out about them yet, so I thought maybe JoJo was just talking big to impress me or something. We stayed there about an hour and then I left. JoJo stayed. I went home and slept."

There was an uncomfortable silence when he finished. Ricky looked at Jay, Jay looked at Collette and then all three focused on Ramirez.

Kirschman finally spoke up. "So it sure as hell sounds like you know who's guilty. Why didn't you just tell the cops your story? Problem over."

"No man!" Ramirez shouted. "He's part of my gang. I give him up and it'll come back to me, and worse, to my family. Anyway, it's mine to carry. All the fuckin' evidence points to me. My car. My bad. I wish I'd stayed home that night. Can you guys really help me?"

Jay nodded his head and said "That's why we're here. You know it will all come out in the trial. If JoJo did it, they're going to find out anyway. Ricky, you have your work cut out for you. Collette, whatever Ricky needs, you're his go to. Ron, you better be sure you've told us everything. No lying, exaggerating or fucking around. Whatever Ricky asks for or tells you is the same as if it was me or Collette."

Kirschman looked toward Ricky and asked if he wanted some time with Ramirez now, which he did. He got up and everyone else stood. Collette motioned to Ricky and Ron to follow her. She took them to an empty office and told Ricky to holler if he needed anything.

Ricky smiled and nodded. "You bet I will," he said, then watched her walk out and close the door.

CHAPTER THIRTEEN

Ricky Burns and Ron Ramirez sat staring at each other until Ricky finally spoke up.

"Ramirez. We gotta get something straight between us, first."

Ron Ramirez sat looking stone faced at Ricky. "Yeah, like what?"

"Don't ever lie to me. Ever! You can lie to your lawyer, you can lie to your girlfriend and your mother but you can't lie to me. You give me any wrong information or lie about anything, when I'm out there trying to save your ass and I find out, I'm done. I need total honesty. I could discount good information or follow bad information if you tell me anything but the truth. This is about saving *your* life."

Ramirez looked him in the eyes and nodded. "I hear you man. I ain't lying. I told you the truth. I didn't kill them."

Ricky looked hard at the football player. "Okay then. We've got work to do, kid."

They spent the next two hours going over every second of the night of the murders. Nothing was too small to mention because anything could lead to something bigger. Burns went over the timeline, and if he could believe their client, he figured there had to be video at the club. He'd also have to track down the guy Ramirez said he took the picture with and just how long he'd been there. Then he'd start searching for witnesses in the area who might have seen something, anything that could back Ramirez' story.

It was dark out by the time they were ready to leave. Ricky was surprised to see that Collette was still there.

"You ever go home?" he asked.

"Once in a while," she smiled. "I stayed tonight so I could give you copies of our files. You'll find everything we have in them. The police reports don't match our client's story though, but I guess that's no surprise. You're going to be a busy man." She winked and flashed that smile again.

"No doubt," he said, knowing she was understating his challenge. "Anywhere around here to grab dinner?"

"Lots of places. What do you feel like having?"

"Steak and potatoes."

"There's a Capital Grille right here on Brickell."

"Sounds good to me," he said. "Hungry?"

"I am in fact."

"Feel like steak and potatoes? I hear there's a Capital Grille around here," he smiled and winked.

"Give me two minutes to close this place up, and you're on."

Chapter Fourteen

Ricky Burns buried himself in the Ramirez files for the next couple of days. Collette was right; he had some serious work to do here. If the football player was telling the truth, and Ricky felt he was, then the cops had it all wrong. It looked like a pretty half-assed investigation on their part. They hadn't looked at any video from the club, just taken the word of a couple of people who said they'd been there that night and were sure it was Ramirez who'd gotten into a shoving match with someone although no one knew who. That was enough to make them hone in on him which they had no problem doing. Ramirez had been on police radar since he was a kid. He had been involved in petty crime, often but as a juvenile he got away with too much. He'd also been linked to gang activity in recent years although they never got anything solid enough to get him off the streets. Once he was drafted by the Demons, he'd stayed off their radar until now.

There was someone or ones who had to have witnessed the shootings. Ricky planned to canvas the neighborhood around the club and the parking lot. He'd spend a few nights around the time Ramirez said they were there that night. Nothing goes down without any witnesses. When he found them, he'd finesse them into giving him something he could use.

He was going to have to talk to JoJo as well. That was going to be a trip. If he was the murderer, he knew he wouldn't get much truth out of him. JoJo set Ramirez up when he had him toss his gun, but Ricky was good at what he did and figured he could trip the little creep up enough to find out if Ramirez was telling the truth about staying at the club while he got the car.

CHAPTER FIFTEEN

It was one of those South Florida days. Not filled with sunshine and quiet waters, but rather gray with bilious dark clouds, plenty of wind and even Indian Creek was rougher than someone living on a houseboat would appreciate.

Ricky figured it was as good a day as any to start chasing some leads. The Club didn't open until nearly midnight so he'd have to start scavenging the streets around it to get a feel for traffic patterns and if he was lucky, maybe find someone who had seen something, anything, that could back up the football player's story.

He drove down to South Beach, parked in the lot he knew Ramirez had parked the night of the murders. The humidity was miserable down here. It didn't matter if it was sunny, cloudy or storming, any normal human sweated. Ricky was no different. The second he stepped out of his air-conditioned car the sweat started dripping and it wasn't even ten in the morning.

The area had deteriorated badly in the '80s. Police cameras dotted the streets to keep an eye on the madmen and criminals. Castro opened his prisons and announced that anyone who wanted to get their relatives should do so. He didn't, of course, give any clue that he was going to force people to take prisoners and leave Cuba. When they landed in South Florida, they found an already dying South Beach and finished it off. Criminally insane refugees filled the desolate streets raising the robbery, rape and murder totals to alarming numbers.

It had grown so far out of control that the Beach Commission finally decided to clean it up, and that's exactly what it did. Lincoln Road, which at one time had been the Rodeo Drive of South Florida, began to come awake again with artists filling the empty stores. The better the area cleaned up, the higher the rents went, driving the artists out and bringing a new generation of boutiques and fine restaurants–and of course, the clubs.

Ricky sucked up the heat and started walking the streets. He wanted to get the layout straight in his mind. Which streets were one-way, which were most heavily traveled. It would be different at two in the morning, of course, but the more he knew about the area the better he could navigate the case.

As the day wore on, Ricky found a small deli to grab a late lunch. He couldn't help but think about Collette's smile and wished she were here with him. He knew he was going to be spending more time with her during this case but he had to get her out of his head for now, which wasn't easy to do. He went over his notes as he ate and started to compile a list of questions in his mind for the people at the club.

CHAPTER SIXTEEN

Ricky was exhausted but it was finally late enough to visit the club and start finding out how much truth their client told and how much was wanna-be fiction. He found the club manager just minutes after he arrived.

Joe Bloom was thirtyish, well dressed and snotty. The man ruled the roost here. Bloom decided who could come in, who'd get VIP rooms and who'd be thrown out. He didn't want to release the videos from the night of the murder to Ricky but took him back to his sleazy little office and said he could watch there. Bloom carefully explored videos until he came to the one Ricky wanted.

"Okay, Mr. Burns. It's set up for the night you want. I can tell you this though. There were no altercations in the club that night, as you will see."

"Thanks," Ricky said, not wanting to get into any further conversations with this prick.

Ricky went slowly through the video, over and over again. Bloom was right, no altercations that night. So where were they getting that from? He did see exactly what Ramirez had described. A guy clearly asked to take a picture with the football player to which Ramirez had acquiesced and smiled for the camera. The first good news. Now he'd have to track that guy down and see what happened outside of the club that night. Unfortunately, there were no cameras monitoring the front door.

Bill Barnes was in the club. Bloom knew exactly who he was as soon as Ricky showed him the video. He rolled his eyes at the job of finding him somewhere in the undulating crowd but told Ricky to come with him. It didn't take but a few minutes to find him. When Ricky explained why he needed to talk to him, he was more than willing.

Ricky asked him about the night without giving away the two versions he knew. Barnes was effusive about the way Ramirez had been so decent about taking the picture. Football players, models and celebrities of every kind were usually in the VIP Rooms. He'd been excited to see his favorite wide receiver out in the open and approached him immediately.

"So he took a picture with you, and then what?"

Barnes thought for a moment, and then, as though he had just remembered, said "Yeah. He didn't stay much longer. In fact, I don't think he was in the club for ten minutes."

That was almost exactly the time the video showed. Nine minutes was all the time he had stayed. So Ricky asked, "Are you sure you didn't see him get into any scuffles? Maybe exchange a few punches?"

Barnes scrunched his face and told Ricky, "No way! He was in and out of here, like I said."

"So that was your only interaction with Ramirez that night?"

"Well, I didn't say that. Um, I kind of went out after he did. I mean, I wasn't kidding when I said he was my favorite wide receiver."

"So what happened outside the club?"

"He was with a friend. When I walked up to thank him again, his friend got a little hot under the collar. He grabbed the keys from Ramirez and said he'd get the car which was fine with me because I got to stay and talk football with Ron 'til his buddy got back. And boy, when his buddy got back, he jammed on the horn as soon as he pulled up. That guy acted like he was on his way to a fire. He left rubber on the street screeching away."

Ricky thanked him. He couldn't have been happier with what he'd learned so far. It fit exactly with Ramirez' story. The bad news was he had to go back out

into the heat—yes, the humidity was as bad at night—
and start walking the streets to find someone who saw
something. There's always a witness. It's just about
finding one.

CHAPTER SEVENTEEN

Ricky started walking from the club, traversing the streets to the car. He bumped into a few people, all knew nothing. Almost to the parking lot, he saw a street cleaner. The guy was moving slowly and meticulously picking up every piece of anything he saw. Ricky approached him, introduced himself and asked about the night in question.

Roberto Martinez was a Cuban refugee who had worked for the City for twelve years. He was a proud older man, anxious to help but clearly reluctant to talk.

Ricky understood. If the old guy had seen what Ricky thought he had, it would only stand to reason he would be afraid. It was starting to get light outside, so he invited Martinez to have breakfast. There was a little Cuban restaurant across the street, already open. Martinez hesitated slightly, and then smiled and thanked him, saying in his broken English he'd very much like to get a bite to eat.

Ricky let him order whatever he wanted, and they both had too many cups of cafe con leche. The street cleaner had seen it all. He described a little dark guy shouting at some people in a car. They got into a scuffle of words and the "little, dark guy," who Ricky knew was JoJo, pulled out a gun and shot the two people in the front seat, maybe someone in the back seat as well. He'd immediately gotten into a black Mercedes and screeched away in the direction of the club.

So there it was. JoJo was the shooter but Ramirez couldn't turn him in out of fear for his family. Ricky made a mental note to keep this witness between him and Kirschman for now. This was going to be a helluva case.

CHAPTER EIGHTEEN

Ricky called Kirschman's office and felt a little shiver when he heard Collette's voice.

"So what's going on, Ricky Burns? Making any headway?" she asked.

"I'm not doing too bad," he said. "And what's with the heat in this town? I've done nothing but sweat every time I leave air conditioning."

"Aw, you'll get used to it. Sunshine comes with a cost," she laughed.

"Yeah, thanks. I'll keep that in mind. I've picked up some good information but I'm not sure how we can use some of it. He wasn't lying about the club. I've seen the video from the night of the murder that the police never bothered to check. I also found the guy he took the picture with. He's good with testifying to the time in the club as well as outside afterwards. He's Ramirez' biggest fan so I'm not at all worried about his testimony."

"Well," Collette responded, "that's a great start."

Ricky laughed. "That's nothing. I found a witness to the shooting and he described JoJo as the shooter. But we have this problem and it's not going to make things easy for us. Ramirez doesn't want to give JoJo up."

"I get it. You want to come in and discuss your next move with Jay? Some stuff has come up since your last meeting so I was going to call you anyway."

"Okay. I need to stay up on everything or I can't do my job. How about sometime later in the day tomorrow, and afterwards, if you're up for it, I'll buy you dinner again."

"That sounds like a plan. How about coming in at four? Jay's going to be in court all morning anyway. You want to pick the place for dinner or trust me to do it?"

"By all means, you take the lead. Make reservations. I'll see you tomorrow."

"I look forward to it," she said, sounding like she really did.

"You know, Collette, so do I!"

CHAPTER NINETEEN

*R*icky spent the next morning researching JoJo Jackson. He knew there had to be something else in his background if he killed those people the way he did. It was an ambush, and he was way too casual about it to have no other record. It didn't take long for him to find something. JoJo shot up an apartment in Liberty City before all this happened. What was that about? He sighed and closed his computer. There was only one way to find out about that little incident; get his butt down to Liberty City and do some sleuthing.

He found the building easily. It still had boarded up windows on the apartment. He learned it belonged to a woman, used his sources to find out her name and number and called her. Sandy Johnson answered on the first ring. She seemed nice enough. He told her why he was calling and asked if she would meet with him. She told him to meet her at the coffee shop down the block from her building in a half hour. He felt like he was finally in business.

Ricky took a seat in the coffee shop facing the door. He waited a half an hour but she didn't show. Another fifteen minutes and he sees two guys walk in the door. Both were big mean looking dudes. One was wearing a jacket, the other a hoodie. In South Florida, in this heat? He knew that couldn't be good. They looked around, saw Ricky seated alone and came over to him.

Ricky, quite sure what was under the jacket and not knowing what was coming, suggested he take off his jacket and stay awhile. The jacket guy frowned and looked Ricky right in the eye. "It's not the jacket you should be worried about, dude."

The one in the hoodie spoke up and asked, "What the fuck you want from my girl, dawg? Whatever it is, leave her out of it and deal with me."

Ricky, anxious to take the temperature down, suggested they sit and have something to eat. They did. Ricky told them he worked for Ron Ramirez and his attorney. "There's no way you'll be hurt in any way by this. I'm probably as eager to get JoJo Jackson as you arc. Let's work together, and anything you tell me stays between the three of us."

DeWayne Rhodes, Sandy's boyfriend, hesitated at first then began to open up, much to Ricky's relief.

"Liberty City is a small area in a big city. So long as we stay in our own 'hood, there's no trouble. JoJo don't understand that. He comes from up North where they play different. He decided he wants to take over my City. That's why he shot up my girlfriend's apartment. People on the street saw it but they're afraid of JoJo so they won't talk."

Ricky nodded. "Well, I'm not afraid of JoJo."

"This isn't the first time he's shot stuff up. He had a beef with someone in a club a few weeks back and shot a guy over it. He's still out walking around and no one's talking."

Throughout their meal, the talk about JoJo continued. The more Ricky heard about JoJo, the more determined he was to get him off the streets. Although he was now a private investigator working for the defense, in his heart he remained a homicide cop. He couldn't just ignore what he was hearing. He had to protect Ron Ramirez, as distasteful as it was for him, but he owed nothing to JoJo.

When everyone finished their meal, Ricky thanked them and paid the bill. It was getting late but he wanted to get to the police before his meeting with Jay. He was considering postponing that meeting until tomorrow when his phone rang. It was Collette. He took a deep breath and answered.

"Ricky? Jay's stuck in court and has to cancel today. Sorry to call at the last minute, but he thought he'd be able to settle out. No such luck though."

"No problem. I've got plenty to do. I think when we meet, I'll have some good news," Ricky responded.

"Jay'll be happy to hear that. We need a break in this case."

"Well, I'm on it."

After a brief silence, Collette spoke. "Uh, Ricky…"

He could picture that smile. "Yes, Collette?"

"I'm still available for dinner."

Ricky thought his heart missed a beat. He managed to respond, "So am I. What time do you want me to pick you up?"

"I'll need time to go home. You know, get changed."

"No," Ricky interrupted, "Don't change. I like you just the way you are."

"Ha ha. You know what I mean. Besides, that way you can pick me up at my house and I won't have to go back to the office after dinner to get my car. It's strictly for my convenience," she laughed.

"Oh, and here I thought you were doing it to impress me."

"I wouldn't mind doing that as well," Collette's voice had taken on a very sensual quality.

It took Ricky a minute to recover his voice but told her that would work for him. She then gave him her home address and he agreed to pick her up at 6:30. He wondered what it was about that woman that made him feel like a kid with his first crush. He hung up and headed to the cops to give JoJo up.

CHAPTER TWENTY

Ricky was feeling good about his findings. He knew the Beach Police would be glad to have the information, and maybe it would help with the Ramirez case. Either way, the cop in him couldn't let this go.

When he arrived at the front desk he showed his credentials and asked to see a detective from the Major Case Unit. The Sergeant looked like he wanted to hear more but recognized that Ricky was focused and not likely to make small talk. He gave directions to Major Case and watched as Ricky hurried away.

A Detective Bill Sewell introduced himself and again Ricky pulled out his credentials. He was a big guy, Ricky figured about 6'2", clean shaven, blondish, good looking and oozing attitude. Ricky explained he was working with Jay Kirschman on the Ramirez case.

Sewell scowled. "That dirtbag? I don't get these guys. They're worth millions but don't think they have to follow the laws. He had his life set."

"Remember," Ricky said, "He's innocent until proven guilty, and from what I've learned, I'm not sure he's good for the murders."

"Yeah, right!" Sewell laughed without humor and looked at the private detective as though he were insane.

"Well, I'm not here about Ramirez so we don't have to debate about him." Ricky didn't want to spend time fencing with the detective. "I do have some information that I'm pretty sure you'll find useful."

"Okay, let's hear it." He rolled his eyes.

Ricky told him what he'd learned about JoJo. He went into detail on the shooting at the building. Sewell advised that wasn't in their jurisdiction.

"Okay. I'll attend to that later, but I figure Club Z is in your jurisdiction, right?"

Sewell said, "Damn right." Now he was interested.

Ricky told him what he knew about the shooting at the Club. He told him JoJo had put the fear of God into all witnesses to both shootings.

"You think my client is a bad guy? JoJo makes him look like a choir boy."

"Well, let's check D.A.V.I.D. for his driver's license and bring him in for questioning," Sewell said, beckoning Ricky to follow. The Driver and Vehicle Data Information Database was invaluable to police. It had everyone's license so all they had to do was type in the name and they had a picture of their suspect.

Ricky watched as Sewell put JoJo's name into the computer which brought up his license almost immediately.

"Gotcha!" the detective called out and printed it. "This is good stuff, Burns. I'll put together a photo array and see if the guy who got shot picks Jackson out. I'll get back to you and let you know how it goes." Ricky smiled and said he was glad to be of help. He handed Sewell his card and asked that he be kept in the loop if possible.

"No problem there. You've given us our first lead on that shooting. You're right. No one has spoken up. Everyone was deaf, dumb and blind that night. I hope your sources are right." This time the attitude was gone and they shook hands with mutual respect.

As Ricky was leaving, his thoughts turned to dinner. And Collette. Tonight.

CHAPTER TWENTY-ONE

Ricky picked Collette up. She told him she'd reserved a table at her favorite sushi restaurant. When she saw his face fall, she asked if that was okay with him.

He hesitated, then said, "I don't eat anything that comes from the water."

Collette pursed her lips and looked into his eyes as if trying to figure out if he was teasing. It quickly became clear he was not.

"Ohhhhh. I guess that rules out my idea. There's a great place on South Beach that has a fabulous salad bar and all you can eat steak, ribs and any other beef you can think of. It's early enough that we can probably sneak in without a reservation."

Ricky smiled. "I hate to ruin your plans…"

"Don't be silly," she interrupted. "It's not really about the food with me. How about you?"

She'd caught him off guard. "Uh, I don't guess it is, now that you put it that way."

"Good. We agree. Meat and salad, again."

Collette was right. They beat the reservation crowd and had a long, leisurely dinner. Ricky told her about his day but other than that their chatter was more about their lives. They found they had a lot in common, including exes. He had two, she had one. They both had kids. They both were single now. There was no doubt they each found the other interesting and attractive.

Just as the conversation was becoming more intimate, Ricky's phone rang.

"One second, Collette. I gotta take this. Sorry."

She smiled, nodded and listened while he spoke.

Ricky hung up and looked into her eyes. "Good news. They got a hit on JoJo. They're picking him up."

"This is going to make my boss very happy, Ricky. You've already started earning your paycheck."

When the bill came, Collette snagged it from the waiter.

Ricky reached to get it from her but she pulled her hand away, shaking her head. "This one's on me."

He looked at her, trying to figure out what she was doing.

"Don't look so confused," she teased. "I have my reason for paying."

"Yeah?" Ricky asked. "And what would that reason be?"

She gave him *that* smile and his knees went weak.

"I want you to feel obligated."

Ricky played dumb. "I am obligated. I'm all in on this case."

Collette laughed. "Oh, I'm not worried about your work ethic."

"I didn't think so, but I didn't want to look like a fool if you were," Ricky said, feeling all in on anything Collette wanted.

"Good," she said. "Take me home…"

CHAPTER TWENTY-TWO

*R*icky was awakened the next morning by Collette. He couldn't help but think that was even better than waking up on his houseboat. He loved looking out at the water first thing but looking at her made him even happier than being on Indian Creek. He smelled coffee.

"I made breakfast. We have to eat and run," she said.

Eating and running was the last thing he wanted to do at that particular moment but the aroma of fresh coffee was calling his name. The night had been incredible. Ricky felt like he'd known Collette forever and he liked that. He hoped she felt the same way.

After the biggest breakfast this bachelor had eaten in a long time as well as three cups of cold brew, Ricky was ready to head into the day. They decided their evening would stay between them. He kissed her full on the lips then left to go home, change and get over to Kirschman's office to discuss the case.

When he got to the office, Collette gave him a big good morning smile and told him Jay wanted to talk to him immediately. There'd been a call from Ramirez, and things were starting to heat up.

"How's it going?" Kirschman asked when Ricky walked into his office.

"It's going," Ricky said. "I've got a lot to tell you but Collette said you've heard something from Ramirez. I'll let you go first."

"That kid is in a rage. Not good. Apparently, JoJo was arrested by the Beach Police last night. Sources tell him he's giving them everything they want to hear about Ramirez to save his own sorry ass. He's lying, of course, but the cops are listening. I'm concerned Ramirez'll go after the little son of a bitch and kill him." Ricky sat quietly for a while staring at the floor. Finally, he looked up and said, "Beach cops work quickly."

Jay looked perplexed. "How so?"

"Well, it just so happens I found a couple of interesting facts about JoJo and his bad acts, so I took the information to them. I had no idea they'd pull him in so quickly, but I figured when they did, JoJo would turn on Ramirez."

"What am I not getting here?" Jay asked, sounding a little pissed off.

"I've got a witness who will testify against JoJo in court. I found someone who saw the shootings go down, and sure enough, he described JoJo, not our client.

I also learned JoJo has his own butt on the line in some other cases of murder and destruction which is why I turned him in. They'll have a tough time proving anything because everyone seems to be afraid of him. Very afraid.

"I talked to a couple of thugs and found out he'd shot up one of their girlfriend's apartments. They would rather have shot me than talked, but I swore I would never bring them into it. JoJo was trying to move into their territory, and the only way he seems to know how to do anything is violently."

There was a knock at the door. Collette stuck her head in.

"Uh, Ron Ramirez is here."

Jay frowned and muttered that he hadn't invited him. Collette nodded and told them he was insistent on talking to them. Jay shook his head and told her to send him in.

Ramirez stormed into the office with fire in his eyes.

"That motherfucker told them where to find the gun! I'm gonna shoot his sorry ass."

Jay stood and told Ron to sit down and cool off.

"You're not going to shoot anyone. We're already trying to get you out of two murders! You need to chill out *now*!"

He sat but did not stop ranting. Jay turned his back on Ricky and Ramirez and stood staring out his window at Biscayne Bay. When the agitated football player finally calmed, he turned back to them and sat down.

"Look, kid, you hired me to do the worrying and I hired Ricky here to do the sleuthing which he is. I'll tell you when to worry. You picked up the gun by the barrel, right?"

Ramirez nodded.

"Okay. They'll have to explain why your prints are only on the barrel if you shot them, and why the handle is clean. The trial will be the time to bring everything out. Mr. Burns has already found a witness. You just gotta trust us."

"A witness?" Ramirez asked. "To the murders?"

"Yep." Ricky smiled.

The three of them sat in silence for a couple of minutes, and then Ramirez stood and said, "Okay. I'm going."

"Stay out of trouble," both Jay and Ricky said at the same time.

"And stay the hell away from Jackson," Ricky added.

"Yeah, count on it," Ramirez assured them.

When the door closed, the attorney and the investigator looked at one another.

"He's going to do something stupid, isn't he?" Ricky asked.

Jay rolled his eyes and said, "I have no doubt."

CHAPTER TWENTY-THREE

Jay Kirschman and Ricky Burns knew their client very well. Too well. Ramirez left Kirschman's office and went on a mission to find JoJo Jackson.

As soon as he learned JoJo made bail, he headed to every place he knew JoJo might go. His mind was racing. No way he was going to let that little fuck testify against him. JoJo gave up where his gun was, now he was going to find out where Ramirez' gun was, up close and personal.

The longer he searched, the more pissed off he got. It looked like he was hiding but not for long.

Maria Gonzalez swore she hadn't seen him. She told Ramirez the cops had come and confiscated her computer early this morning. She tried to reach JoJo, but he wasn't answering her calls.

JoJo must have told them that Ramirez had searched for information on her computer about the murders. Another mark against him. He'd find the little traitor, somehow, some way. He wasn't answering Ramirez' calls either.

It took a couple of days but Ramirez found JoJo in a pool joint. JoJo winced when he saw him but gave him a big smile and invited Ron to join the game. Ramirez refused and told him he needed to talk to him away from here. JoJo hesitated but saw the look in his old friend's eyes. He knew he had to follow him out of there.

As soon as they were outside, Ron put his arm around JoJo too tightly to make him believe something good was coming. Ramirez half-dragged him to his car, opened the passenger door and pushed him in. Ramirez was in the driver's seat before JoJo could open the door and run.

The two men rode in silence. Ramirez was headed for the Everglades. JoJo worried that he was going to throw him to the gators. Not quite. When they got to a clearing, Ramirez stopped the car and turned to a frightened JoJo.

"Get out of the car, man."

"Whaddya want, dawg?" He asked, trying to look as though he wasn't in fear for his life.

As they got out of the car, Ramirez shouted, "You set me up and put the cops onto me, you sorry little fuck! You know what I want," Ramirez said, his face twisted in an evil stare.

"No, man. I didn't say nothin'," JoJo whined.

"Fuck you didn't. You think I don't have my ways of finding out shit you done? Think again, man. You think I fucked you before? You don't know shit about getting fucked!"

With that, he pulled the gun out of the back of his pants, aimed and shot him in the side of his head and was stunned to see the bullet fly out of his right eye. JoJo stumbled backwards, not believing what was happening. Ron left JoJo screaming for help. As he drove off he thought to himself, *I should have shot him a second time in his thick head*, but he was certain that one shot had done the job. JoJo was a dead man and would never be found."

CHAPTER TWENTY-FOUR

The next day the texts started arriving.

3:00pm *JoJo Yo the crazy part about all this is u did that bullshit for no reason n me being the real friend i was to u i didn't try to ruin u even after you tried to kill me think how real that is so i was the real friend at the end of the day n the tears should be in my eyes after you betrayed me. i never crossed u but i loved u n no way n the only reason u got to rock me is cuz we was so a hundred. i never thought ud be the one to shoot me n thats real talk. i would never try to frame u. u left me with one eye and a lot of head trauma u owe for what u did n its too bad u don't know me enuff to know that this convo is private between us aint no lawyer or cop to see. we both know what happened and u needa pay up and dont tell me u can't pay. u so paranoid made u do the shit you did to me. i go to the police u be done for nigga.*

4:30pm *Ron I love u and u r not gonna frame me for some bread and thanx for the info he'll be getting reached to! Always will love u cuz u were my brother n u kno hat but hope the best for u.*

And so they continued, resolving nothing. Ramirez was crazed with anger at the thought that his buddy was trying to frame him and was now trying to blackmail him after setting him up for murder. JoJo would never see a penny of his money. In fact, he thought he should have taken out both eyes.

That one-eyed bastard couldn't sue him. He knew well that JoJo would give him up, which is what he planned to do anyway if he tried. Meanwhile, he couldn't tell Kirschman or Burns what he'd done. They clearly weren't kidding when they warned him not to do anything. Fuck 'em. *An eye for an eye* he thought, and laughed out loud.

He'd gotten rid of the gun and knew it would never be found. Ramirez' attorney would deal with the gun JoJo had him toss, so even if he did try to bust him for the loss of his eye, no one would ever believe him. If they did, they'd never be able to prove it.

CHAPTER TWENTY-FIVE

Ricky arrived at Kirschman's office about 10:00 the following morning. Collette greeted him with a quick kiss on the cheek and told him Jay was waiting for him. Ramirez was already there.

Jay stood as he walked in but Ramirez did not. He sat there looking sullen and mumbled a begrudging hello. He was going to get a lot more unhappy as the morning progressed.

"Well, I've gotten some news," Kirschman said. "I'm not going to go into my sources but I will tell you hospitals have to report gunshot wounds to the police, Mr. Ramirez."

"What that's got to do with me, yo? I ain't got no gunshot wounds."

Ricky sat forward and looked from Jay to Ramirez. This was the first he was hearing about any hospital reports.

"It would appear that JoJo showed up at Jackson Memorial with a bullet in his head, right through his eye last night. He refused to tell the cops who did it. Made up some shit about getting caught by a wild shot in the 'Glades. You have anything to do with this, Ramirez?"

"Fuck no, man. Why you think I did it? I told you I wasn't going to do nothing and I didn't." His voice was raised in protest and he glared at Jay.

Ricky was pissed. "You stupid punk! We told you to keep your nose clean and stay out of trouble. You went after JoJo and shot him after telling us you'd steer clear. What is wrong with you?"

Ramirez stood now. "I'm telling you it wasn't me. Why you think I did it? You're supposed to be defending me not finding more shit to blame me for!"

"Sit down." Jay wasn't too happy either. "We think you shot him. He's not giving you up, so what's going on?"

"I dunno. JoJo pisses folks off all the time. If I'd of done it, I'd of done it right and he'd be dead."

It got quiet in the room for a couple of minutes, then Ricky turned to Ramirez and in a low, measured tone said, "Listen, you little thug. I might be working for the defense now, but the first part of my adult life has to count for something. Anything, I mean *anything* else happens to that guy–I don't care if he's struck by lightning–I'm done with this case. I won't allow you to wage a vigilante war while you're facing a trial for double murder. Not on my watch anyway."

Kirschman's brown eyes were dark and wide and he looked disgusted. "Listen Ron, I'm behind Burns one hundred percent. It's going to be a motherfucker to get you off on the two murders you're charged with already. You do what we tell you, no deviations from the script. You got that?"

Ramirez grunted. "Whatever."

"No, not 'whatever.' Try Yes, sir." Jay shouted.

Ricky just sat there glaring at Ramirez. Jay shook his head and told Ramirez to go home and stay there. Ramirez slowly stood, looked at his attorney and investigator, not even attempting to hide his hostility.

"Okay. I'm outta here, but I'm not staying home."

Ricky stood up at this point and told him he could stay wherever he wanted but to stay away from anyone involved in this case and not shoot anyone else.

When the door to Jay's office closed, Ricky sat down and turned toward the lawyer. "You know he did it."

Jay nodded, "Yeah. It's not like he's above it. Shooting his good buddy in the head just because he's selling him out and going rogue. I hope he never turns on us!"

"Listen, Jay, I meant what I said to him. You might be used to working with these dirtbags but I'm new at this. I spent too many years chasing bad guys to look the other way when someone I'm trying to help goes nuts and starts shooting people. If it happens again, I'm outta here, and taking my retainer with me."

Jay smiled weakly. "I hear you. I represent lowlifes, but I don't condone them trying to kill others while I'm trying to save their asses. He does anything else and you and I are both done with him."

Ricky asked if there was anything else he needed to know before he left. Jay assured him he was caught up on everything.

"Okay. Then I'm going to do some detective work and see what I can find out about JoJo. The cops have him, and I have no doubt they're going to cut a deal to get Ramirez."

Outside of Jay's office, Collette was busy at her desk but stopped and looked up at Ricky.

"All good? It got a little loud in there," she said.

"It's as good as it's going to be, I guess. I hate this. Ramirez is a piece of work, bad work. I took the job though, so I've got to find out what JoJo's telling the cops and what the cops are going to do about it. You free for dinner?"

"With you?" she asked.

"No, with Ramirez. Of course with me," he said.

There was that smile. "Absolutely!"

Ricky felt good for the first time since he'd walked into the office.

"Okay. I'll call you later."

CHAPTER TWENTY-SIX

Ricky Burns headed back to the houseboat. He had phone calls to make and didn't feel like doing them from his car. Besides, his office overlooked the water and a little of that might help to cool him down. He'd known that eventually, if private work was his destiny, he'd have to work with the element he'd spent all those years taking off the streets. Yet he hadn't anticipated clients to be running around shooting witnesses. Worse, Ramirez wasn't just a witness, he was the murderer. It boggled his mind that someone like Ron Ramirez could be that stupid and make millions of dollars because he could play a game. Didn't football players need some smarts? There was a bad taste in his mouth that went all the way to his stomach.

Once on the boat, he went straight to his office, sat down at his desk and stared out at Indian Creek. The water worked its magic and calmed him down enough so he could start making notes. First, he was going to have to call Bill Sewell. He felt as though he'd made a friend there, and since he'd arrested JoJo, he might share some of what he'd learned.

When they met this time, Sewell was cordial and had no problem sharing what was going on with the case. He told Ricky he'd been correct about the guy. He was a badass.

"Did you know someone shot him?" he asked. "In the head right through his right eye."

"Yeah, I heard. He say who did it?" Ricky asked, saying a silent prayer it was someone other than Ramirez.

"Nah. He's not talking about it at all. He is, though, talking about Ramirez."

"Don't believe a word he says. The guy's full of shit and only out to save his own ass." Ricky warned.

"Yeah, you would say that. He's looking to trade information about the Ramirez murders to get a plea deal. In fact, he's giving us the gun your client allegedly used in the shootings."

"Is he now," Ricky asked, smiling broadly. Well, I'll tell you what you're going to find on that gun, if you're interested."

"I'm interested." Sewell cocked his head.

"You'll find Ramirez' fingerprints on the barrel. The rest of the gun was wiped clean. According to my guy's account of the night, the gun was in the car when

JoJo picked him up from the club. Little one-eye had Ron throw it out of the car. He told Ramirez he'd had a little altercation over drugs. It never occurred to the genius that he was being set up, but he did have enough sense to pick it up by the barrel to toss it."

"I'll let you know after we pick it up and run some tests. Just be aware he's hot to cut a deal, and it would go a long way to convicting your football player for a double murder."

"I don't think so, but we'll see soon enough. I actually believe Ron about the murders. Your guy is going to have to cop a lot more pleas before this is over."

"Listen Ricky, you and I get each other. You do good work. You were able to get people to talk when it was a bust for us. We wouldn't have JoJo if not for you, but for that very reason, you need to watch your back around here. Plenty of the detectives resent a private investigator nosing into our cases. Worse, you're a former New York cop, which as far as they figure is attitude and trouble. It'd be their pleasure to make you look bad."

"Thanks for the heads up. I'll try to make myself scarce. Besides, I've got my own case to prepare."

The two shook hands and Ricky left feeling pretty good about the visit.

CHAPTER TWENTY-SEVEN

On his way home, Ricky put in a call to Kirschman. Collette answered. "Hi Ricky."

"I love caller ID. Personal greetings are so special," Ricky laughed. I just left the Miami Beach Police. They picked up JoJo for that club shooting and he's trying to cut a deal by giving up Ramirez. All he's got is the gun though, and that'll work in our favor at the trial. I say that based on our client's statement, assuming he's telling the truth.

"It's coming together for us. I've got that street cleaner who is going to testify he saw JoJo, not Ramirez. The gun is good, too. Sewell told me JoJo wouldn't give up whoever shot him, so there's something going on there I'd like to find out about. If JoJo did it, why isn't he saying. I mean, he's ready to finger Ramirez for the double murder, but won't sell him out for shooting him in the head. That's screwy…"

"Unless," Collette interrupted, "he wants something from Ramirez. I don't know what, but maybe money?"

"You might have something there. Ramirez got twenty-four million in advance and I'm sure JoJo knows it. The whole world knows it, I'd bet. JoJo's out on bail. Let's hope our jock doesn't find out. If it was him and he shot the guy in the face, I'm thinking he was shooting to kill. I don't want him taking another run at the poor little one eye guy."

"Ouch. One eye. that's harsh," Collette let out a long breath.

"That's what Sewell told me. Shot clear through his right eye. Amazing it didn't kill him."

"You need to talk to Jay?"

"Nah. You can tell him what I got. I'm going home to start putting my witness list together. Figure out what else we need for trial."

"Well, I guess that's it for now. Good talk."

"Collette, did I say I was finished?"

"It surely sounded like it."

"Almost, but not quite. Ever slept on a house-boat?"

Collette giggled. "Never."

"Would you like to see what it's like?"

"Sure. Will I get dinner?"

"Absolutely. And dessert."

"Oh, now there's an offer I can't refuse. I won't get out of here until after six."

"No problem. I'll wait 'til you get there to order the pizza."

"Pizza? I thought you'd be cooking for me."

"Believe me, doll, you'd much rather have pizza. Since my last divorce I've lived on Chinese, pizza, anything that delivers. Would you rather Chinese? I can even get you sushi if you prefer."

"No. If you're not cooking then pizza works for me. The dessert better be good though," she warned.

"Oh baby, I promise, but don't let my past performance give you any expectations," he laughed.

"Too late," she responded, "My expectations are already high."

They hung up and Ricky stepped on the gas to get home. He had to clean up and get that living room presentable although he wasn't planning to spend much time in it.

CHAPTER TWENTY-EIGHT

The next morning Collette and Ricky had coffee then she left for work. He was feeling energized, though not because he'd gotten any sleep. He sat at his desk making notes on what he had to do next. The trial was in a couple of weeks. He needed to lock in his two witnesses and have them meet with Jay for a little review of the facts and to prepare them for what they would be hit with at trial.

His biggest concern was with Roberto Martinez, his eye witness. The man's English was broken at best but he understood the language well. Kirschman would have to spend some time with him. The guy had to be prepared because Ricky knew the prosecution would pounce on him and try to make him screw up.

He wasn't so worried about Bill Barnes. He was well spoken and a big fan of Ramirez. He'd be anxious to score some points with the wide receiver. Ricky figured prepping Barnes would not be a problem.

Then there was the gun. They hadn't gotten back the results on the fingerprints, but he didn't need Sewell to know they belonged to Ramirez. Assuming, which he was not big on, Ramirez was telling the truth, the prints would only be on the barrel. He had no doubt JoJo would have wiped it clean. It would be up to the prosecution to explain why the only prints are on the barrel. He put in a call to Bill Sewell to see if the report was back. It was. Sewell confirmed the only prints were Ramirez's and only on the barrel. Sewell cautioned Ricky that was a non-issue. They had plenty of other evidence. Ricky laughed and told him they had more.

"Ha! Don't get cocky. We might surprise you," Sewell warned.

"Never happen," Ricky shot back.

Just after he hung up, Ricky's phone chirped. A message from Collette: *Jay wants to start meeting with witnesses ASAP.*

He smiled. Kirschman was on the same page. His instinct was to call her back, but it occurred to him that the reason she'd texted rather than called was because she was with her boss. So he texted back: *On it. Give me a date and time and I'll be there with one.*

He put in a call to Bill Barnes who answered on the second ring. Ricky explained that the trial was coming up and he'd need to meet with Ramirez' attorney for prepping. Barnes was cordial and anxious to do whatever he could to help. Satisfied with his response,

Ricky told him it might be short notice, but he'd let him know the date and time. He also offered to pick him up and drive him. Ricky Burns was not one to leave things to chance.

As for Roberto Martinez, Ricky would go to his home and explain what was going to happen. He was concerned the prosecution would try to get their hands on him once the witness list came out. There wasn't much they could do to mess with Barnes. That guy was on a mission to save one of his heroes, but Martinez, not so much. He knew the little man was frightened and that made him vulnerable to hungry prosecutors. If it had been Ricky's call, he'd put the guy in a safe house until he had to testify. Roberto Martinez would not be one to miss work though, but so long as he went to work, he was out on the streets and fair game for everyone.

Ricky glanced at Indian Creek. The water was so still it looked like glass. He yawned and thought, *this is the life.*

CHAPTER TWENTY-NINE

*R*icky drove to the address he had for Roberto Martinez. The shabbier Hialeah got, the closer he was to the old guy's house. It was a small brick home with the only manicured lawn on the block. He might be poor but the old man was proud. Ricky parked in the driveway and knocked on the door.

"*Momentito, por favor*," came from somewhere inside.

He knew Martinez was widowed and lived alone. As he was glancing around the area, the door opened and Martinez stood there looking perplexed.

"Hey Roberto! Remember me? Ricky Burns? We had breakfast awhile back."

"*Si*, yes. You are the policeman I talked to about shootings."

"Yes I am," Ricky said. "Except I'm not a policeman, I'm an investigator. May I come in for a minute? We need to talk."

Martinez motioned for him to come in. Ricky didn't hesitate. It took a minute for his eyes to adjust from the bright sunlight outside. The small living room was dark with heavy curtains covering the windows. The furniture was old but well cared for, and the place was as clean as any he'd ever seen.

Martinez told him to sit and asked if he could bring him a drink. Ricky declined and told him the trial for Ron Ramirez was coming up soon. He'd have to meet with the attorney for some help with his testimony.

"I only talk truth!" Martinez insisted.

"I'm sure you do, but the other attorneys are going to try to confuse you and turn your words into something you don't mean to say. This attorney will help you recognize when they are trying to turn you around."

"I know what I see. Nothing can make it wrong."

"You'd be surprised. I think I'm pretty smart and they've played me. If I can get screwed up, so can you. They will probably try to talk to you before the trial. You don't have to talk to them. They'll try to scare you but you have my phone number and if anyone approaches you, you just tell them you have nothing to say, then call me. In the meantime, go on with your life and I'll call you, pick you up and take you to the meeting with the attorney. You understand?"

"I'm an old man, but not so stupid. I know what you are telling me. I am not afraid to tell truth."

Ricky left but was bothered. Martinez was a good man and he clearly wanted to do the right thing. He'd have to look out for the man and make sure police and prosecutors didn't try to turn him. He was an honest man, but the prosecution would work him over pretty solidly. And then there was that little son of a bitch JoJo.

CHAPTER THIRTY

Another day passed before Ricky heard from Collette or Jay. He was lying in bed enjoying the slight sway of the boat. It rained last night and the creek had not yet settled. Rain on Miami Beach was different than it had been up north. Rain here rattled the windows and boomed with thunder. Occasionally a bolt of lightning would slash so close to his floating home he was sure it would hit. After the rain, the air smelled clean and the sky grew bright with sunshine. He never wanted to go back to New York. All New York had for him were his ex-wives, and they were exes for a reason or two. His children were there but they were old enough for their mother to put them on a plane to visit. In fact, after this case he planned to invite them down for a stay. He missed his kids more than he thought he could. He didn't miss his exes though, not even a little. He didn't have to think about them except when he venmoed their monthly checks. Even that was too often.

CHAPTER THIRTY-ONE

*W*itness lists were exchanged. Ricky was more concerned than ever about Roberto Martinez. The old man called him earlier and told him a policeman came to talk to him. Worse, although Ricky thought he'd warned him strongly enough not to talk to anyone, he apparently saw the badge and felt he couldn't refuse to talk to a cop. The poor guy was one of the few left in the world who actually respected authority. Ricky assured him it was okay but told him once again he didn't have to speak with anyone, cops included. From what he said, he hadn't given anything away. They talked for a while and although the conversation was somewhat worrisome, he didn't believe any damage was done.

He put in a call to Kirschman's office to set up an appointment to meet with Martinez and start prepping him for the trial.

Collette picked up on the first ring and gave a cheerful, "Hi, Ricky!"

"I'm going to have to get a burner phone so you won't know it's me. I like having the element of surprise," he chuckled.

"I'll give you an element of surprise," she laughed. "What's going on? You need me or Jay?"

"Want or need?" Ricky teased.

"Oh, I love to be needed but being wanted is so much sexier!"

"I guess we'll talk about what I want later tonight. I was looking for Jay but you're actually the one I guess I need to speak to."

"So speak."

"You know the street cleaner who gave me the ID on JoJo?"

"Yes, the older Hispanic man, right?"

"Right. Well, a cop got hold of him and asked questions. Although I told him to speak to no one, he thought he was required to speak to the police. He says he told him what he told me. He showed him Ramirez's picture and he said he didn't recognize him. Thankfully, he didn't tell him who he did recognize. I want to get him in with Jay quickly. They're going to do a number on him when he's testifying and I want to be sure he's not going to be tripped up."

"Oh, wow. What about the guy from the club? Anyone approach him?"

"If they have, he hasn't spoken to me about it. I don't expect any problems with him. He's clean cut and literate. His testimony won't be a problem. He's coming to praise Ramirez, not to bury him."

"Okay then. Tomorrow too soon to bring him in?"

"The sooner the better."

"How about 11:00?"

"I'll be there with him in tow. Now let's talk about how much I want you and set a time for tonight." The words just came out. Well, he figured, she flirted with him all the time, so what's good for the goose...

CHAPTER THIRTY-TWO

*R*icky Burns mumbled about the traffic in Miami as he navigated the jams on his way to get Roberto Martinez. The heat wasn't bad enough, but the roads were a bigger clusterfuck than New York. At least he had the houseboat, and time with Collette. This case was as difficult as any he had worked in his career. He knew if they got Ramirez off, he'd have more work than he could handle. Because of that, he was trying to make peace with his new world by staying in air conditioning whenever possible.

Ricky arrived at Martinez' little home. He felt like hitting his horn for the old man so he didn't have to get out of the cool of his car but forced himself to go knock on the door. Martinez answered the door wearing a suit and tie. Ricky thought it must be his only one. Ricky was in jeans, sneakers and a button down shirt untucked.

"Mr. Martinez, you're looking sharp today," Ricky smiled.

"Thank you, sir. Is good enough to wear to the courtroom?"

"Absolutely," Ricky answered. "We're not going to court today, though. We're going to the attorney's office to talk about what will happen at the trial. You need to know some of the questions you might be asked. The prosecution is going to try to turn your story around and you must be prepared."

"But Mr. Ricky, I tell you already that I speak only truth."

"Oh, I believe you, but you've never been on a witness stand before so we're going to walk you through what could happen."

"The policemen came to my house yesterday. I tell them I no have to speak to them. They said I do because they are police. I tell them go away or I call the police to make them leave."

Ricky laughed and asked, "You told the police you would call the police?"

"*Si,* yes. I did wrong?"

"Did they leave?"

"Oh yes, right away."

"Then you didn't do anything wrong. They aren't visiting you because you're their friend. You did the right thing, *Senor Martinez.*"

Martinez looked proud of himself.

They arrived at the law office and Collette greeted them with her usual smile. Ricky's knees went weak every time she did that. He introduced Martinez and asked if Jay was ready for them.

"Just about," she responded. "May I get you gentlemen some coffee?"

"Thanks, kiddo," Ricky said. "Just cream, no sugar for me."

"Like I don't know," Collette shot back at him. "And you, Mr. Martinez? A cup of coffee?"

"You have *cafe con leche,* Missus?"

"No, sorry. I can order some from the restaurant downstairs, though, if you'd like."

"Oh *por favor*, please, no trouble for me."

"Really, it's not a problem. It'll take a little while for them to get it up here, though." Collette not only knew the importance of this witness but she was taken by his old world manners. "I'll bring it in to you when it arrives. Meanwhile, Mr. Burns, you know where the coffee is, go pour yourself a cup."

"Oh, it's 'Mr. Burns now, is it? Did I say something wrong?" Ricky asked, a little perplexed.

"It's called being professional," she snapped back. "You can get your own coffee while I call up for our client's *cafe con leche* and then I'll take you to Mr. Kirschman. Does that work for you?"

Ricky couldn't help but think she looked awfully good as a professional but she looked good regardless of where she was or what she was doing to him.

"Why yes, Ms. Collette. It works just fine." He walked toward the little kitchen in the back of the office, biting back the urge to tell her he'd tell her how it worked for him tonight.

CHAPTER THIRTY-THREE

*A*fter they were seated and pleasantries had been exchanged, Ricky showed a photo array of six pictures to Martinez. They had to be sure that JoJo was in fact the little guy he'd seen the night of the murders. Without hesitation Martinez pointed right to the now one-eyed little bastard. Both Jay and Ricky breathed a huge sigh of relief.

Ricky was still thinking of the cops who continued to hassle Martinez. He was getting pissed about it and made a decision. He'd call Bill Sewell and tell him to call off the dogs.

"Listen, Roberto, I'm going to take care of your problem with the police bothering you. If anyone, and I mean *anyone*, cops, attorneys, whoever, contact you, call me immediately. You comprehend?"

The little man stared down at the floor for a good minute and finally spoke.

"Did I do wrong?" he asked.

"No," Ricky responded, "You've done nothing wrong. I don't want them bothering you before the trial. They know better but they think they can intimidate you to make you see things their way."

"I never lie. I tell you this all the time."

"We know that, Roberto. You we trust. The cops and the prosecution, not so much." Ricky looked to Jay, who was nodding and looking pleased.

"I agree," he said. "You're fine. You know who you saw. You'll be able to pick him out for the attorneys in trial, and that's that. Listen to Burns though. You really don't have to talk to them. We'll back you up on that."

Ricky stood and asked if there was anything else they needed to cover. Jay shook his head and thanked Martinez for his honesty and willingness to help.

"What about the other guy, Barnes? We need a meeting with him," Jay asked.

"Nah, I can handle him. He knows not to speak to anyone, and thankfully, Ramirez is his hero. He'll be good. Nice looking guy. I'm expecting him to be an excellent witness. I'll bring him in if you want to talk with him, though," Ricky said.

"Not necessary. I trust your judgment," was the response.

"Okay. Roberto, let's get you home."

"Yes, thank you sir." He rose and they went into the reception area where Collette was typing away. She stopped as they got to her desk, and asked if the *cafe con leche* was good. Martinez gave her a big smile and assured her it was just the way he liked it. Ricky figured even if it tasted like it was from a sewer, this kind man wouldn't have complained.

"Roberto, go on ahead to the car. I'll be out in a minute," Ricky directed. When the door closed, he glanced down at Collette. She looked at Ricky, cocking her head in a seductive way. "Will you be calling later?" she asked.

"I don't know. I don't want to spoil you," he laughed.

"Fine. I have plenty of things to do without you tagging along anyway."

"Don't get feisty, Ms. Collette. If I do call, will you drop the Mr. Burns and use Ricky again?"

"You can count on that," and flashing that signature smile whispered, "Ricky."

CHAPTER THIRTY-FOUR

Ricky went directly to the Beach Police Department after dropping his charge off. The desk Sergeant saw him and grunted, "He's in his office."

"How do you know who I want?" He didn't like this guy.

"I know all about you, Burns. You're looking for Sewell, right?"

"I guess news travels quickly around here. Yeah, I'm looking for him. Thanks."

He headed back to Major Case and saw Bill as soon as he walked in. Sewell saw Ricky as well and waved him over.

"What's going on, Burns? You have more information for me?"

"I have nothing but requests."

"Requests? What can I do for you?" Sewell looked perplexed. "Your guy's going down y'know."

Ricky smiled. "I wouldn't count on it. I'm really good at what I do."

"So, what are you looking for from me now?"

"Roberto Martinez."

"What about him?" Sewell knew what was coming.

"Look man. I don't want to step on your toes with JoJo, and I certainly don't want your guys stepping on Martinez' toes. How many people are you going to throw at him to try to influence his testimony?"

"What's your problem? We're not breaking any laws. He's going to testify for the defendant. Fair game."

"C'mon, Bill. Enough is enough!"

"I like you, Burns, but I gotta tell you, things are heating up for your boy. Giving me JoJo was a gift. You're good at what you do so I know you'll find everything out without me telling you, but our case just gets better and better."

It was what Ricky had been concerned might happen. "He flipped, didn't he?"

"Yep, and he didn't waste any time."

"What'd they offer him?"

"Sweet deal. Five years and he's out, and he gets to stay out until the trial is over. Just another good citizen, giving up what he knows about a really bad guy…"

Ricky laughed out loud. "Oh yeah. Great guy. He's a lunatic is what he is. You better hope he doesn't kill anyone else before the trial."

Sewell glared at him. "He won't. You better keep your hoodlum football player under control 'til we go to court as well."

"My hoodlum football player is innocent. I can't say he isn't a hoodlum but I know he didn't kill those guys. I did hear that JoJo had another altercation and lost an eye over it. You know anything about that?"

"Funny you should mention that. I asked what happened. He gave me some fucked up story about being in the 'Glades and getting hit with a bullet. Never saw who shot him. I don't believe him but he wasn't about to tell us anything."

"I'm not buying that story either but I'd sure like to know who did it. I have some suspicions but nothing I can prove, or want to…"

"Interesting. Listen, Burns. I think you're a good man and I'm sure you're a great investigator. I'll talk to my people and see that they don't have another go at your witness. I'll leave it to the prosecution to eat him up and spit him out."

"You're too good to me, Bill. I'd appreciate it, really. Can you stop them from hassling my other witnesses as well?"

"I'm not making any promises, but I'll see what I can do. The trial is soon enough and you know the State Attorney's all over this. It doesn't look good for Ramirez, though, like I said."

"Yeah. You've got so much to hit him with. A gun with prints only on the barrel. A murderer who's being paid handsomely for his testimony. I'm impressed."

Sewell laughed humorlessly. "May the best man win."

Ricky laughed out loud, and said, "I will."

"I'll walk you out. You want to grab some lunch?"

"Promise not to talk shop?"

"I won't if you won't," Sewell said, and the two headed to a deli.

CHAPTER THIRTY-FIVE

Bill Sewell suggested they walk to the deli which was only a few blocks away. Ricky started sweating at the thought of it and offered to drive.

"Everything down here is valet parking. It'll cost you ten bucks."

Ricky laughed. "You're used to this suffocating heat. I'd rather pay the ten bucks."

"Have it your way, man. Ten bucks is ten bucks though," he warned.

It was a small deli with big thick corned beef sandwiches which both men ordered along with french fries. When the sandwiches arrived, Sewell got serious.

"Burns," he said, "I want to go off the record with you."

"Off the record? What are you talking about?"

"I know some shit that I'm very sure you don't. We're in a much better position than you think."

"Okay. I'll bite, off the record. What've you got?"

"Jackson and Ramirez are closer friends than you think."

"Closer than I think? I don't think they're close at all anymore. One eye is testifying against our client to save his own butt. Ramirez isn't feeling much like embracing him. I'd wager to say he's feeling more like beating the crap out of him."

"That may be, now, Ricky, but in the past they've shared more than just meals."

"Will you stop talking in code and say what you mean?"

"You were warm when you mentioned Ramirez 'embracing' Jackson."

Ricky swallowed the bite he'd just taken, looked hard at the detective and said, "You aren't saying what I think you're saying, are you?"

"You've got it. They've shared more than just gang activities together."

Ricky sat dumbfounded. He shook his head, then laughed, "Nice try!"

Sewell's face reflected no humor.

"He's way more credible when he talks about sharing blow jobs and whatever else men do with men. I'm telling you, they were intimate."

"I talked to Jackson's girlfriend. He's not gay! I'd bet Ramirez isn't either. What are you trying to pull, Bill?"

"You can't be that naive, man. I'm not jerking you around here. They started out experimenting and decided they liked it. Gratuitous sex, I swear to you."

Ricky put down his sandwich and let out a huge sigh.

"A football player and a gang banger. Doesn't that beat all! So I guess you think that's going to make JoJo look more credible? I think it gives Ramirez a big break."

"How do you figure that?"

"Cuckolded lover. He's clearly trying to put my client away because he dumped little one-eye. Great big, handsome football player left him. If he's enjoying the sex with Ramirez, maybe women don't give him the same, um, thrill? You've got nothing there."

"I guess we'll let the jury be the judge of that," Sewell grinned.

Ricky rolled his eyes, picked up his sandwich and said "This is really lean corned beef. I'll definitely be back for more, ten dollar parking or not."

CHAPTER THIRTY-SIX

That night Collette arrived at the houseboat bearing gifts. She'd prepared a steak dinner for their evening. Ricky's first home cooked meal in longer than he could remember.

They didn't talk shop through the meal. Collette sipped a Jameson's and ginger ale and Ricky slugged down a couple of Balvines.

"You trying to get drunk?" Collette asked.

"It's been a day," Ricky complained. "Just need to unwind. You and this incredible meal are a good start. The Balvine is to help me relax."

"Do you want to talk about it?" Collette asked, looking concerned.

"No. But I will."

"I don't want to force you," she said. Losing patience, she asked, "You met with that detective again?"

"Oh yeah. I surely did. He went off the record with me about our client and JoJo. I don't know whether to believe what he's saying, but we'll need to prepare to deal with it in the trial."

"There are always hiccups in murder trials. You know that."

"Sure, but not this kind of hiccup. It seems that JoJo and Ron weren't just friends."

"I don't get it. Are you talking about their gang association?"

"No. We knew about the gangs. We didn't know they were sexually involved."

Collette spit out the drink she'd just taken. "C'mon, Ricky. Just tell me what's going on. Don't be funny."

"Nothing funny about it. Just one more thing to deal with at trial time, although, I don't think he'll be able to get it into evidence."

"You're not kidding, are you?" she asked, incredulously.

"Not even a little. Sewell thinks that gives JoJo more credibility. I don't. It'll be better for our case if they find a way to get it heard. They want to bring sex into it, we'll say JoJo is a scorned lover trying to get back at his football playing boyfriend. Along with the gun and Martinez' and Barnes' testimony, JoJo's going to be a real sorry little man. If we can pull it off, the next trial will be JoJo's."

"Jay's going to love this. The kinkier trials get, the more he enjoys them," she giggled. "He's had some pretty wild clients but this mess might be the most interesting."

"I just hope it all goes our way. I never take a win for granted."

They finished their meal in silence. Collette got up and started taking the dishes into the kitchen. Ricky loaded the dishwasher while she wiped down the table. When they were finished, Collette gave him a warm hug which he wasted no time returning.

"Don't worry. Jay's almost as good at what he does as you are at what you do. It'll work out. He's going to love this new twist."

Ricky felt better already. He'd never fallen so fast and so hard, not even with his wives. Collette started to pull away. He tightened his grip.

Raising an eyebrow, Ricky asked, "Where do you think you're going, Ms. Collette?"

"Well, Mr. Burns, I'm glad you asked." She smiled up at him, took his hand and led him to the bedroom.

CHAPTER THIRTY-SEVEN

*R*icky walked into Jay's office at about eleven the next morning. Collette was at her desk. He bent down to give her a peck on the cheek.

"Did you tell him?" he asked her.

"No way! It's yours to spring on him. I'm going to sit in on this meeting, though," she laughed. "Come on, Jay's expecting you."

Jay was sitting in his big leather chair facing his window, not his desk. Ricky figured he'd probably be doing the same if he had a view of that Bay.

"Ricky's here, boss. I'm going to take notes," Collette said as she sat in one of the plush chairs.

"Jay. Good to see you again. It's been at least a day. I've got some stuff though, so we need to talk." He sat down next to Collette.

"Hey Ricky. With the trial getting close we'll probably be seeing a lot more of each other. What've you got for me?" Jay asked.

"I met with the good Detective Sewell yesterday. I think we've bonded. We had lunch at a great deli and he opened up to me off the record."

"Off the record, huh? Must be good stuff."

"That depends," Ricky said. "Good is relative. It could work to our advantage, though, if he manages to get the judge to allow them to enter it."

"If it works to our favor, I'll fucking help him get it into evidence!"

"I'll let you be the judge of that." Ricky looked at Collette who was smiling from ear to ear.

Jay saw the look that passed between them and wondered if something might be going on. "You already told Collette?"

"Uh, well, she's need-to-know, right?" Ricky asked.

"Yeah. Good old need-to-know Collette. I didn't think you'd been out there that long waiting for me."

"Boss!" Collette snapped, "I plied him with coffee and broke him. He had to tell me." She laughed.

"Whatever," he responded. "So, Burns, how about sharing it with me now?"

"Not a problem," Ricky said. "She does make a mean cup of coffee, though." Another look passed between them and Jay sat there nodding. It sure looked like something was going on.

"Okay, spill it, Ricky."

Ricky took a deep breath and began. "Well, you know what good friends JoJo and Ramirez were before all this began?"

Jay cocked his head, waiting for more.

"They were a whole lot better friends than we knew," Ricky continued. "They had a sexual relationship going."

Jay furrowed his brow, and asked "With whom?"

"That's the thing. It's not with 'whom', it's with each other."

Silence filled the room. Jay looked at Ricky. Ricky looked at Collette, Collette looked at Jay.

After he'd digested what he just heard, Jay spoke out. "How do they think they're going to get that into evidence?"

"I have no idea," Ricky answered, "But as far as I see it, it's a gift to us. They want to claim there was a sexual relationship, we can cry that he's a jilted lover trying to get back at the man who got away."

"Interesting take. I don't know why they'd even want to bring that out. I guess their thought is that even though they had an intimate relationship, JoJo came forward and turned him in. Ha! His testimony is bought and paid for by the prosecution. I plan to make sure the jury knows that. I'm feeling better and better about this case."

"That's good to hear," Ricky said. "I like to go into a trial with no loose ends."

Collette cut in, "Loose ends? With you and Jay working the case? I don't think so."

"Well, let's not get too cocky. I just hope the surprises stop coming." Jay looked uncomfortable.

"What's wrong, boss?" Collette grew concerned.

"Nothing really. Things just keep happening that aren't expected. I can't believe those guys were lovers. Always the complications."

"It'll work out. I've got a good feeling about this," Ricky assured him, and rose to leave. "Hey, I haven't seen any ballistic reports yet. Have you heard anything?"

"No. We should have had that by now, though."

"That's good. It means bad news for them. They're hiding the reports for sure." Ricky gave Jay a thumb's up."

"I'll have Collette set something up for us a couple of days before the trial. We can tie up any loose ends then."

"There won't be any loose ends," Collette said softly as she got up to walk Ricky out.

Jay Kirschman watched his paralegal and investigator walk out of his office and thought "Yeah, there's something going on."

CHAPTER THIRTY-EIGHT

Time always seemed to move more quickly as a trial grew near. Ricky spent his days going over his files and making sure he had missed nothing. His evenings were spent with Collette, either at her place or his. The case was tough but something good comes out of everything, and for Ricky, Collette was the best. He was constantly impressed with her intelligence, insights and abilities.

He asked why she hadn't become an attorney rather than a paralegal. It was a money thing, he learned. She'd planned to go to law school but had loans to pay back for college and she planned to go to work, save and eventually start taking law classes at night. Her first job was with Jay Kirschman. She loved working with him. He gave her so much responsibility. She'd tell people she was the office attorney and Jay did trials. Jay told her she was better than a lot of the attorneys he'd worked with, especially when he was at the Public Defender's office. So she'd never gotten around to law school. Jay thought she was so good that he offered to pay for her to go to law school.

"I told him he blew it," she laughed. "He was ready to put me through law school and bring me in as a partner. I gave it serious thought but working with him taught me that my strength was in research and dealing with clients."

She took a breath and said, "But this is the first time I've gotten involved with an investigator. I like it. Anyway, I've sat through enough of his trials to recognize I wasn't cut out for that part of lawyering. I couldn't do what Jay does in a courtroom. He's incredible."

"Well," Ricky said, "some people go through their entire lives without knowing what they want or they work in jobs they hate. And Jay's right. You are great. I saw that the first day I was in your office."

Collette chuckled. "You're just saying that because you're crazy about me."

"Wrong! I mean yeah, I'm pretty taken with you, but I'm not just telling you this because of that. You're the assistant that every boss wants. Today? Hard to find."

"Aw, thanks, Ricky," she cooed. "Want me to show you how awesome I am on a houseboat?"

She didn't have to ask twice. Ricky got up from the sofa, took her hands, pulled her up, and they headed for the bedroom.

CHAPTER THIRTY-NINE

Ricky arrived at Kirschman's office at nine the next morning. They were meeting to talk over strategy and prepare Ron Ramirez for trial. He was not looking forward to dealing with the football player today. The guy just rubbed him the wrong way. He found himself struggling to hold his tongue whenever he spoke with him.

"Hey Mr. Burns," Collette and that smile.

"Hello Ms. Collette. Good to see you again."

She lowered her voice and said, "Like you didn't get out of my bed this morning. Yes, nice to see you as well." They both laughed.

"Jay here yet?"

"Are you kidding? He got here at the crack of dawn. Files are all over the place in his office. Looks like he might have even pulled an all-nighter. Give me a sec, I'll tell him you're here."

Ricky watched her go into the inner sanctum, thinking about last night. She was back in a flash, waving him in. She was right. The office was askew with files and Jay looked like he hadn't slept.

"Morning, Ricky. Ready for a fun day?"

"Oh sure. You know how much I enjoy meeting with Ramirez. The punk."

"Yeah, but he pays well. We're going to have to confront him with JoJo's accusations. You know that'll play well with him. We've gotta do what we've gotta do, though."

"Did you get any sleep last night?" Ricky asked.

"I dozed on the sofa. Just a catnap. I'm good though. Collette went to Starbucks and got me a couple of cold brews. Fixed me right up. How about you? Did you sleep?" A wicked grin spread across his face.

Ricky cleared his throat and looked hard at Jay. Could he know? *Nah* He thought. "Oh yeah. I don't have a problem sleeping regardless of how big a case is."

"I'll just bet you don't," Jay shot back. "I'll bet you don't!"

"Did you want to get down to business or continue discussing our nights?" Ricky asked.

"Yeah. Yeah. Ramirez'll be here any minute. You ready to have a go at him?"

"More than ready. How do you want to handle it? We can go over what he should expect, let him talk, ask questions, although he probably won't because he thinks he knows it all, then hit him with JoJo's story?"

"Yep. Sounds like a plan."

Just then Collette peeked into the office and told them Mr. Ramirez had arrived.

"Send him in, Collette."

"You want me, too, or should I sit this one out?"

"I want you in here for the briefing, then I'll think of a reason for you to leave when we hit him with the sex. He'll be upset enough without a woman being in the room."

Collette opened the door wider and turned to the client. "Come on in, Mr. Ramirez. They're ready for you."

The football player entered, scowling. "We need to do this for real? My story ain't gonna change."

"You're paying me to decide what you need to do and what you don't need to do. You think you can do it all by yourself, feel free. I keep the retainer."

"Don't go getting your balls in an uproar, Kirschman. Whatever you say, I do. Have I not followed all your directions 'til now?

Jay glared at his client. "I don't know about that but I can't prove you haven't. Sit your ass down and let's get to work."

The meeting went on for hours. When it came time to hit Ramirez with the JoJo thing, Jay sent Collette to order lunch. Once she was out of the room, both Kirschman and Burns turned to Ramirez.

Jay spoke first. "Listen kid, you know JoJo has flipped and has fingered you, but you don't know everything he's said. You need to know, though, and so do we."

"What you talkin' about, yo?"

Ricky spoke up. "We're talking about your relationship with him."

"We got no relationship now. Little one-eyed bastard lost me! He thinks he can finger me for his murders and get away with it? Not happening."

"It's a little more complicated than that, Ron. No, a lot more complicated."

"Complicated how?"

Jay shot a look at Ricky, and Ricky took his cue.

"You like women or do you prefer men?" Ricky asked.

"Fuck you, man. Women, of course."

"Wrong answer, Ron. At least according to JoJo," Ricky continued.

"He don't know nothing about the women I go with."

Both Kirschman and Burns got quiet. The thought was that if they let him ramble on, it would all come out. A couple of minutes went by before Ramirez started ranting. When he quieted down, Jay asked, "You ever had sex with JoJo?"

"Fuck no."

"Ron, you can't wish this away. JoJo told the prosecution you and he have had a sexual relationship for years. You going to deny that?"

"Fuck you, Burns! Fuck you both. I'm out of here." With that he got up and slammed out of the office.

"Collette!" Jay yelled.

She rushed into the office immediately.

"Jay!" she shouted back. "Where was Ramirez running off to? Or from? Running away from JoJo's allegations?"

"That's exactly what he's doing. Denied any sex with JoJo. He's a real heterosexual man," Jay said sourly.

Ricky laughed, "Yeah, he's the man alright."

"Text the prick and get him back here pronto. Tell him if he doesn't get his bad ass back here in ten minutes, I'm done."

"I wonder which one is lying, Ramirez or one-eye. On it, boss." She headed back to her desk.

While they waited, Ricky and Jay strategized on how to handle Ramirez when he returned, which they knew the jock would. They decided to stand pat on what they'd revealed and let Ramirez deal with it. They had to get ahead of it before it came up at trial.

Jay's door opened and Collette stuck her head in to say their client had returned.

"Send him in, please."

"Sure, boss," she grinned.

The football player walked into the office with the same nasty look he'd left with. "What up? You wanna turn me into a gaywad or what?"

"We don't want to turn you into anything. We're just repeating what we've learned. Did you screw around with him or not?" Jay asked.

"Man, I let that little fagot blow me one time. He's the one who gets off sucking dicks, not me. One fucking time!"

"So, you don't consider that sex? Who do you think you are, Bill Clinton?" Ricky asked.

"Hell no. Put a paper bag over anybody's head, man or woman, and I'll let 'em blow me. He knew what he was doing ,too, so he's probably done it with plenty of guys. Big shot gang member."

"And you swear you only had one episode with him?" Jay asked.

"Episode? It wasn't even an episode. One and done!"

Ricky spoke up. "Is there anything else we should know? Any other people who could surprise us next week?"

"Looks like you guys have dug up everything. I got no secrets left. They gonna say that at the trial? Make like I'm a fagot, too? What am I supposed to tell my fiancé? She don't know about it. Nobody but that sonofabitch knew until now."

Ricky advised him to tell her soon and get it over with. "Make it a no big deal like you did to us. Just a blow job."

"She don't even like to give me blow jobs. This isn't going to go well."

"If we can keep it out, we will," Jay answered. "Far as I'm concerned, it's got nothing to do with the murders. I can't guarantee it won't come out though, so you better prepare her. And Ramirez, you've got to get a hold of that temper. They're going to hit you with all the stuff we talked about earlier and then some. I don't care how badly they piss you off, you stay calm. I won't let you take the stand if you can't handle it."

"Maybe I'll smoke some dope before the trial. That ought to calm me some," Ramirez laughed.

"Oh yeah. That'd be all we need."

About an hour later, after Ramirez was gone, Jay called Collette in so the three of them could caucus.

Ricky cocked his head and asked whether the ballistics report on the gun had come back. It hadn't.

"If we don't get it before trial, I'll move for it at trial."

"You know if they aren't sending it, it's in our favor. I'm feeling really good about this," Ricky smiled.

"I am, too," Jay responded. "I am, too. Let's call it a day."

"Ricky and Collette both rose. As they left Jay's office, he watched. "Yeah," he thought, "They're doing the wild thing. Collette's even starting to sound like him."

CHAPTER FORTY

The Sunday before the trial, Ricky spent the morning going over his files. They needed to get the ballistics report because he had no doubt it would prove it was the same gun that shot up that apartment building in the City. Everything else was pretty much in order. Kirschman had been working nonstop. Ramirez and the witnesses were keeping a low profile for which he was grateful.

Collette arrived at the houseboat in the afternoon with a bathing suit.

"It's such a great Beach day. Since we can actually walk across Collins Avenue and be there, I thought I could drag you away from the case and get you to relax, take advantage of our wonderful climate."

"Wonderful climate, huh? You mean hot box, I think."

"We'll go for a swim, lay on the sand, watch the surfers and just rest. You won't be disappointed."

"Okay. I haven't even seen the beach except when I cross the causeway, and I really am ready for tomorrow. Get changed and I'll put on my trunks."

Ricky was sitting in his office wondering what took women so long to change clothes when Collette walked in wearing a bikini. A string bikini. It took him a few moments to catch his breath.

"I thought you said you brought a bathing suit."

Collette cocked her head, put her hand on her hip and asked, "What do you call this?"

"I call it something that makes me want to take you to the bedroom rather than the beach. Wow!"

She laughed and grabbed his arm. "C'mon, Ricky. We'll enjoy the beach and when we come back you can ravish me until the trial."

"I never ravish before a trial."

"Maybe I can convince you *after* the beach," she put her arms around his neck, leaned into him and kissed him hard on his mouth.

When she let go, he stood back and said, "That's not a way to get me to the beach but it could make me change my mind about ravishing before a trial."

"Okay, beach first, bed next." She started for the door with Ricky following right behind her admiring her butt.

CHAPTER FORTY-ONE

Ordinarily Jay Kirschman would have never gone to trial without the ballistics report on JoJo's gun; however, he decided to wait until the trial to request it. Assuming his client was telling the truth, the report would not only show that the gun killed the two people Ramirez was accused of murdering, but it was also the same gun that shot up the apartment building in the City. He chose to wait until today to bring up the fact that a copy was never supplied. He had the element of surprise this way.

The Judge was announced and everyone stood. The Honorable Calvin J. Jones would be presiding over the trial. He was a white guy's white guy. Jay was not happy this was the judge that was the overseer. He was a known bigot and had a lousy Bar rating.

At the prosecution table were two of the toughest Attorneys in the State. William Green was first chair. Almost 6'5" with a mop of gray hair and angry dark eyes, he was known for his ability to turn even the strongest witnesses into bumbling fools. Second chair, Janet Prentiss was nicknamed Sharkie by defense attorneys. She was reed thin with dyed shoe polish black hair and a habit of looking down her sharp nose when she addressed witnesses, while managing to look almost benign to jurors. Both were shrewd, worthy adversaries.

Ron Ramirez sat quietly between Collette and Jay at the defense table. It was the first time they'd seen him looking scared. Jay assured him he had everything under control. If Ramirez followed directions and kept his temper in check, it would all go well.

The bailiff stood and said, "All rise. The Honorable Calvin J. Jones presiding."

Judge Jones called the Court to order. The room grew immediately silent. Jay stood up and asked for a sidebar. The Judge did not look happy but beckoned all the attorneys to the bench.

"Your honor. We received the fingerprint report from the prosecution but we never got the ballistics. I respectfully request a copy before we begin."

"Judge," Green snarled, "We gave them everything."

The Judge glared down at Jay and asked what his problem was.

"Your honor, we never received that report. We believe it contains important evidence and we need a copy. I'd be happy to submit an affidavit swearing to the fact we never received it, if that would help."

The Judge admonished the three attorneys to work it out or he'd handle it his own way.

Green looked at Jay and said, 'I know we sent it to you but in the spirit of cooperation, I'll give you another copy." Shaking her head, Prentiss walked back to the prosecution table and started going through files.

"That work for you, Kirschman?" the Judge asked.

"Yes, Your Honor."

"Okay. As soon as the prosecution finds the report and turns it over, we'll begin."

"Thank you, Your Honor," Jay turned back to Collette and Ramirez, smiling.

Colette nodded. Jay sat back down with her and Ramirez to wait for the report that he knew would be one of the most damning pieces of evidence they had. He hoped. If it confirmed his suspicion that it was the same gun that shot up the apartment building in Liberty City, they were a quarter of the way to a win.

The Courtroom was packed with both fans of the beleaguered football player and family of the dead. The room was silent while everyone waited for the next step.

Prentiss pulled a piece of paper from the files and walked it over to Jay. She smirked as she handed it to him and whispered under her breath that it wouldn't get him anywhere.

Jay looked up at her and said, "So why did you hide it?"

"We didn't hide it. I was sure we sent it to you. Must have been lost in your office. Whatever. Now you have it, let's see where it takes you." She turned on her heel and headed back to her seat.

Kirshman turned to Collette and told her he was going to have their guy check the gun out as well. "Never know what the State might have 'missed'."

CHAPTER FORTY-TWO

Opening Argument – Prosecution, William Green

Ladies and Gentlemen of the Jury. I'm William Green, and I stand before you today to tell you about a ruthless murderer. I'll be brief because talk is relatively cheap, especially when we have so much evidence.

Yes, Ron Ramirez is a famous football player. He's worth millions. But don't let his fame blind you to the fact that although he had everything going for him, popularity, money, and a career that most men would cherish, it wasn't enough. Ramirez grew up in a tough area, and despite his prowess as an athlete, chose to hang out with gang members and guns. Football gave him a way out, but off the field he wasn't able or didn't want to give up the lifestyle he'd known as a poor street kid. He had the chance to get out of the life, but instead of taking it he chose to take the millions of dollars he was making as a player and hang with hoodlums.

We will present evidence, including first person testimony that will prove Ron Ramirez' guilt without a shadow of a doubt. He went out to a club on South Beach, got into a scuffle and left angry. He then brutally and without remorse shot and killed two innocent people and didn't look back. He tossed the gun which we found covered with his fingerprints. No other prints were found on it. Only the prints of Ron Ramirez.

He went to a friend's house immediately after the murders, used her computer and searched for news about the murders. There's no way he could have known about what happened that night if he was innocent. Don't be blinded by who he is on the football field.

Ron Ramirez, football hero? Perhaps, but not that night. It's important to separate the man from the wide receiver. Being great on the football field does not mean he's a decent man off the field. In fact, he hung out with thugs because he is a thug.

The evidence will back us up, That's a promise.

Thank you for your time and attention.

CHAPTER FORTY-THREE

Opening Argument – Defense, Jay Kirschman

Good morning, ladies and gentlemen. I represent Ron Ramirez, and I plan to disprove everything the Prosecution told you about him. They spun a great story but none of it is true.

No, that's wrong. Two things you were told are true. The first is that Ron Ramirez' prints were the only ones on the gun. I'll explain that during the trial. The other thing that was correct was Mr. Ramirez used a computer in an attempt to find out what happened that night. There is a reason for that, but not the one Mr. Green gave.

The State attorney is also right about something else. Mr. Ramirez did hang out with thugs, and one of them is their key witness. We'll get into that and him during the trial.

We want you to listen to this case with an open mind. Listen to what the witnesses have to say and look at each piece of evidence presented with an open and clear mind.

At the end of this trial, I know you will find that Ron Ramirez did not do this crime, not just beyond a reasonable doubt, but beyond a shadow of a doubt.

Thank you for your time and attention.

CHAPTER FORTY-FOUR

The Prosecution's Case

Thomas Blair

The first person called to testify was Thomas Blair, the uniformed officer who examined the crime scene. Blair was a short, stocky man, with red hair and a ruddy complexion. He testified he'd been on the job for eight years and was a veteran in responding to murders, rapes and robberies. A decent cop with no citations for bad behavior or outstanding contributions, he appeared weary as he took the stand. He was expecting to answer the usual questions and go home to catch some sleep.

William Green walked him through the details of his investigation. Blair confidently went over the murder scene. It was in the wee hours of the morning on South Beach. The area in which the murder took place was deserted when he arrived. He found two Black men dead in the car. They had each been shot several times. There was also someone else shot but still breathing No evidence was found. It was his opinion that it was just another drug deal gone bad. He called the Crime Scene Unit and an ambulance for the man who was wounded. Then he waited until they arrived, filled them in on what he knew, then left. He'd not been involved in anything further to do with the case.

Kirschman asked a couple of benign questions, and reserved the right to call him at a later time. He got back to the defense table to see Collette speaking heatedly with Ramirez.

"What's going on?" he asked.

Ramirez spoke up and growled that he thought Jay would be more aggressive.

"I'll get more aggressive when it's called for, Ron. Are you trying this case or am I?"

Colette said that's what she'd been trying to tell him. "Thanks, Jay." She turned to Ron and asked if he "understood now."

"Just settle down, Ron. There's a lot to come, and I'm in this to win," Jay said. "And keep your voice down. The last thing we need is for the jury to see you acting out and thinking you're a hot head!"

Ron lowered his head and muttered something unintelligible. Jay nodded, "Good. Then we understand each other."

Janice Blaine

Crime Scene Unit

Janice Blaine was a hottie, at least that was Kirschman's first impression as he watched her slow, sexy walk to the stand. He felt bad that he was going to have to take her apart on cross-examination.

Green walked toward Ms. Blaine and introduced himself. She nodded, and he asked what she found when she arrived.

"Two dead Black men. They'd been shot several times each. It appeared as though the gunfire had come from outside the car. There was a third man who was wounded but breathing."

She continued to relate that she'd seen it all before. Probably a drug deal gone bad or a gang revenge killing. There were no witnesses and no one else was around except two the two EMTs who were loading the wounded guy into the ambulance. She'd asked them for a couple of sheets before they left the scene. Once they were gone, she went over to the car, covered each of the bodies with a sheet and called for a tow. She had the car taken to the impound lot with the dead bodies inside.

When Green said he had no more questions, Jay stood then walked toward the witness. He smiled at her and introduced himself. She smiled back but would not be smiling for long.

"So, let me make sure I've got this straight. You got to the scene, surveyed the area, identified the bodies and confirmed they were dead. Am I correct so far?"

"Yes. They'd been shot several times."

"Did you dust for prints?"

"I didn't feel it was necessary. There was no evidence that anyone came near the car. It was getting closer to morning traffic and I wanted to get it cleared so we wouldn't end up cordoning off the street and holding up people trying to get to work."

"So, you're saying you were more concerned about a morning traffic jam than you were about the two Black dead men in the car?"

Green jumped to his feet, "Objection! Counsel is interpreting, not following the facts.

"Your Honor," Jay responded. "There was no search, no dusting for prints, and she's worried about snarling up the morning traffic. It sounds to me like it was just another two African American men killed over drugs or a gang feud, so she covered them up, left them in the car and had it towed. Who tows a car with bodies still in it? Unless, of course they think it's just another couple of Black men working a drug deal.'

The Judge looked over his glasses at Jay, then at Green and shook his head. "Try not to interpret the motives of the witnesses, Mr. Kirschman. That's why we have a jury.

"Sorry, Your Honor, but it sure sounded to me like she was more concerned about the morning traffic than she was about finding some kind of evidence," Jay said and turned back to the hottie in the witness seat.

"Watch yourself, Kirschman," the Judge warned.

"Okay, Ms. Blaine. No evidence was found at the scene. No witnesses around. You determined it was either a drug deal gone wrong or a gang slaying, and had the bodies towed, in the car they were murdered in, to the police impound lot. That pretty much the way it happened?"

"Yes," she replied.

"How many other crime scenes have you found dead bodies in a car where you've had the car towed with the dead men in it?"

"None" she responded as she looked right through him.

"So you contaminated the crime scene by leaving the bodies and evidence to bounce around the car?"

Green again, "Objection! He's putting words in her mouth.

"Sustained."

"So tell me this," he continued. "Did you canvass the area for witnesses?"

"I told you. It was late and no one was around."

"So you didn't canvas the area that night. Did you go back the next night to see if anyone was around who might have witnessed anything?"

"No."

"Did you go back at all to survey the area for anyone who could have seen the shooting go down?"

"No."

"I guess it wasn't important enough to follow up? Just another couple of Black drug dealers who got popped."

"Objection!" Green was on his feet again.

"Sustained. Mr. Kirschman, try to avoid the narration." The Judge looked pissed.

"Did you find anything at all at the crime scene that is directly related to Mr. Ramirez?

"No."

"Okay. No further questions. I reserve the right to recall the witness."

Maria Gonzalez

Green called JoJo Jackson's girlfriend Maria Gonzalez next. She looked very uncomfortable and was sweating in the cool courtroom. The woman was extremely nervous.

"Ms. Gonzalez," Green started, "You look a little shaky. Would you like some water?"

She shook her head. Green reminded her that when he asked her questions about the case, she'd need to speak up. "No nodding or shaking your head. Court reporter needs to record your answers."

Maria nodded, and caught herself, "Yes, sir.'

"I just have a couple of questions for you. Relax. In the early morning on the date of these murders, did you receive any visitors?"

"Yes."

"Who?"

"My boyfriend JoJo and his friend Ron."

"That's JoJo Jackson and Ron Ramirez?"

"Yes sir."

"Do you see Ron Ramirez in this Courtroom today?"

"Yes sir. That's him,' she said pointing at the defense table."

"During that visit, what occurred?"

"Well, JoJo and I, we were, you know, messing around, and Ron was on the computer."

Green nodded. "What was Mr. Ramirez doing on the computer?"

"He says he wants to check out a, you know, shooting on the Beach."

"Did he say how he knew there was a shooting on the Beach? Was he involved?"

"He just said he thought something bad had gone down and he wanted to know what it was."

"How long did the men stay with you?"

"JoJo, he spent the night. Ron took off after he finished on the computer."

"Did he find what he was looking for?"

"I dunno. He just left. He didn't even say good-bye. He was pretty upset about something."

"JoJo didn't know what was wrong?"

"He say Ron must've gotten himself into something, but he didn't know what it was."

"So JoJo didn't seem to be upset?"

"Uh uh. He was all lovey dovey and looking to get to the bedroom. Um, I guess I shouldn't say that…"

"Just say it the way it happened. We're looking for the truth here."

"That's what went down. JoJo stayed and Ron just took off."

Green thanked her and she started to get up. The Judge told her to stay where she was because Mr. Kirschman wanted to ask her a few questions as well. She immediately sat back down and what little color she had left on her face disappeared. She was white as a sheet.

"Hello, Ms. Gonzalez. I'm Jay Kirschman, Ron Ramirez' attorney. I won't take much of your time. You look a little pale. Are you okay?"

"I guess so. I never been to court before."

"Well, there's nothing to be nervous about. Just answer my questions truthfully."

"Okay."

"So we've established that JoJo and Ron showed up at your place in the wee hours of the morning. You said JoJo was his usual self but Ron was upset or angry?"

"He was. All he wanted was to get onto my computer."

"Did he say why?"

"Uh uh. He didn't say nothing."

"And JoJo had no idea what his friend was looking for?"

"Just that there was some trouble and he wanted to know if it was on the Internet yet."

Green jumped to his feet, "Objection. Hearsay!"

"Sustained." The Judge then looked at the young woman cowering on the stand and said, "You can only testify to what you saw Mr. Ramirez and Mr. Jackson do, not what they said."

"Yes sir, Mr. Judge."

Jay asked, "So at that time you didn't have any idea what Mr. Ramirez was searching for on your computer, Ms. Gonzalez?"

"That's what I told you."

"Where's your computer now?"

"The police took it."

"They took it?"

"Yeah. I don't have no computer now. They said I have to wait till all this mess is over before I get it back."

"I see. Okay. Thank you for your cooperation." Then he turned to the Judge and said, "No further questions."

Green stood immediately and said, "Your honor, I'd like to call JoJo Jackson as my next witness."

The Judge looked at the clock, paused for a minute and said, "I think this would be a good time to break for the night. We will start with your witness first thing tomorrow morning. Court is in recess until 9:00 a.m. tomorrow."

The Bailiff stood and told everyone to rise as the Judge left the courtroom.

CHAPTER FORTY-FIVE

Jay, Colette and Ricky decided to grab dinner together and have a couple of drinks to relax. Some attorneys hole up in their office and review files in preparation for the next day's questioning, but not Jay Kirschman. He prepped like a maniac prior to a trial but during a trial, he didn't worry. If something unexpected came up, he dealt with it at the trial. His preparation was so thorough that there were rarely any surprises he couldn't handle by winging it.

The three went to a small out of the way place that offered great food, oversized drinks and a quiet corner. No one spoke for a few minutes while they finished their first drinks. Jay motioned to the waiter for a second round, and Collette was the first to speak.

"So, I thought it went pretty well today."

"I think you're right," Jay responded.

Ricky looked at the two of them and said he'd like to hear about it. He'd spent the day babysitting their witnesses and was anxious to know how far they'd gotten and what was next.

"Nothing unexpected," Jay said between sips of his drink. "They put the detective who covered the shooting on the stand. He was no help to them.

"Then they put Janice Blaine, their crime scene tech on. She was a fucking gift to us. Actually, they both were. I can't remember a shooting I've seen handled this badly."

"I wish you could have been in there with us," Colette bragged. "Jay took them both apart easily." Then, looking at Jay, "I thought Green would bust a gut when you made your remark about them being racist."

"You called them racists?" Ricky asked Jay, eyes wide.

"Not really. I just implied the reason the investigation was so shoddy was because they wrote it off as just another couple of Black thugs who got popped in a bad drug deal. Which is exactly what they did.

"The only witness they put on that could have hurt us in any way was JoJo's girlfriend. She was adamant that Ron had gone right to the computer when they arrived. She made JoJo look like innocence personified, while telling them Ron was upset and looking for the murders—although at the time, she didn't know exactly what he was searching for or what he found. Nothing we can't undo when we put on our case though."

"Who's up next?" Ricky asked.

"JoJo Jackson. I'm really looking forward to that little shit getting on the stand. There's nothing he can say that we can't refute."

"When do you think they'll be finished?" Ricky asked while cutting into his steak.

"I don't know, but it shouldn't be longer than a day or two."

The three finished their meals and agreed to meet the next morning at the Courthouse. Jay paid the bill and asked Collette if she needed a ride back to the office.

"I already have one, thank you," she smiled.

Jay looked at her and then at Ricky, and said, "I thought so," and headed to his car.

"Who's your ride, Colette?" Ricky was smiling.

"You, big guy. Who else?"

CHAPTER FORTY-SIX

Prosecution continues

JoJo Jackson

"*A*ll rise for the Honorable Calvin J. Jones," the Bailiff droned.

Once he was seated and everyone had settled, Jones told Green and Prentiss to call their next witness.

"Thank you, Judge. JoJo Jackson will testify next."

JoJo took the stand and was sworn in. Jay was impressed at how he cleaned up. He was in a gray suit, his tight curls were cut short and he was clean shaven. Too bad he had a dark brooding look and that sinister eye patch. Jay leaned over and whispered to Ramirez and Collette, "This guy has no idea what's going to hit him after he lies his ass off under oath to Green."

Green asked him to go over the night of the murders in as much detail as he could remember. Just as Jay had predicted, JoJo started with a lie. He railed on about how Ron was in a bad mood all night and had gotten into a scuffle with someone at the club.

"We had to get outta there because Ron was in a mood," JoJo complained.

"Do you know why he was 'in a mood'?"

"He just gets that way. He thinks he better than everyone else now that he's a big shot football player making millions."

"So he had a bad attitude. What happened?"

"Some guy bumped into him and Ron he started pushing him. Then the guy shoved back. Ron said we should get outta there because it was too crowded and he couldn't get a VIP room." He stopped and looked at Green.

"Okay, Green responded, "So what did you do then?"

"I followed him out of the club. I stayed there while Ron went to get his car." He paused again, looking to Green for what was next.

"And did he pick you up?"

"Yeah."

"Go ahead…"

"He was having a fit about something. I think he got into it with some druggies or something and he was pretty riled up."

"Anything else?"

"He had a gun on the console. When we got away from the club, he tossed it out. I could smell it'd been shot, but he wasn't saying nothing."

"Where did you go from the club?"

"We was going to Prime 112 to get something to eat but it was already closed."

"Then what?"

"I said we should go to Maria's, uh my girl's house, and she'd feed us. So we drove there but as soon as we got in, he run to the computer and starts looking for something."

"Do you know what he was looking for?"

"Yeah."

"And what was that?"

"He was looking to see if anything was on the Internet about whatever happened near the club."

"Okay. Did he find what he was looking for?"

"I dunno. He just tore outta there when he finished. He was in a mood, man. Bad."

"Afterwards, did you find out what happened?"

"I sure did. Two guys were killed near the parking lot Ron's car was parked in."

"Did Ron tell you about it?"

"No. We saw it on the television news. I guess he killed 'em."

Jay Kirschman stood up and objected. "Your Honor, the witness is speculating about something he has no intimate knowledge of."

"Sustained. The jury will disregard the witness's implication that the Defendant had any part in the murder."

Green turned and smiled smugly at Jay who glared back at him. He'd clearly prepared JoJo Jackson carefully on what to say and how far to go.

Turning back to JoJo, Green asked, "Have you had any contact with the Defendant since his arrest for those murders?"

"No."

"He's made no attempt to talk to you?"

"Uh uh."

"You were such close friends. Did you reach out to him after he was charged?"

"No. He didn't call me either."

"No further questions."

JoJo immediately stood to leave the witness stand and the Judge told him to sit down. "Mr. Kirschman has some questions for you."

Kirschman stood and walked over to JoJo.

"Hello Mr. Jackson. How close were you and Mr. Ramirez before this incident?"

"We was real close. We been friends most of our lives."

"If you were that close, why didn't you reach out to Mr. Ramirez when you learned he'd been arrested and charged with murder?"

"I dunno. I got enough of my own problems. I didn't want any part of it."

"You were with him the night it happened. You said he threw the gun out of the car window, right?"

"Yeah."

"Did you go to the police?"

"No. I told you, he's my buddy."

"So how did the police learn about your involvement?"

"I wasn't involved, yo? I just happened to be with him that night."

"You've been arrested before, right?'

"Yeah."

"You've been arrested quite a few times, five times maybe?"

"Yeah. I been arrested lotsa times. So what?"

"Did you get arrested for shooting up an apartment building awhile back?"

JoJo started to say no, when–

"Objection! Mr. Jackson's not on trial here."

"Sustained," the Judge growled.

"I'll withdraw the question." Then turning to the witness, "You've also been convicted of battery?"

"Yeah."

"You resisted arrest–to the point where a police officer was hurt badly, as well

"Objection!"

"Overruled. I'll allow the question. Answer it, young man."

"Yeah."

"You were also convicted of robbery with a firearm, weren't you?"

"Yeah."

"When you were convicted of robbery with a firearm, did you give the police your real name?"

"Not at first."

"So you don't always tell the truth, do you?"

Both prosecutors stood and objected. "Argumentative!"

"Sustained. Jurors will disregard that question," Judge Jones directed.

"Okay, then. You were recently arrested for shooting up a club and injuring one of the patrons, isn't that correct?"

"Yes." JoJo lowered his head.

"And didn't you make a deal with the prosecution to testify against your good friend for less time in jail?"

JoJo looked over at the prosecution at this point. Getting no reaction from either prosecutor, he mumbled "Yeah."

"Wasn't that the same gun that was used in the murders that are the subject of this trial?"

"No, man. I used my own gun."

"I know you did."

Green stood and objected again.

"Sustained. Let's leave the commentary to the witness. You ask the questions, Kirschman."

"You were actually the one who got the car when you left the club that night, weren't you?

"No!"

"And when you got the car, you got into a beef with the murder victims, and in fact, you are the one who shot and killed them…"

"Objection!" Green shouted.

"Sustained!"

"You shot them with your gun."

"Objection!"

"Counselors, come up here. Now."

The three attorneys went up to the Judge. After a short, heated conference, the Judge told the jurors to disregard Kirschman's last question.

"As you were driving away from the club, you testified that Ramirez threw the gun out of the window toward the right side of the road."

"Yes."

"It's a little strange that Ron's fingerprints, from his right hand, were found only on the barrel of the gun, but not on the handle or the trigger, don't you think?"

"Objection! The witness is neither an expert in ballistics or fingerprints!"

Confident that he'd asked everything he wanted the jury to hear, Kirschman said "No further questions at this time, but I reserve the right to recall the witness at a later date."

Judge Jones asked the prosecutors if they had any further questions. Janet Prentiss stood and walked toward the witness.

"Mr. Jackson. Did you shoot those two men?"

"No."

"That's all, your honor." And Prentiss headed back to her seat.

Detective Cameron Evans

Ballistics Expert

Once the Courtroom settled down after questioning JoJo, Green called Cameron Evans to the stand.

"Detective Evans, how long have you been with the MIami Beach Police Department?

"Twelve years."

"How long have you been assigned to the ballistics unit?

"Five years."

"Over those five years how many guns would you say you have you examined?"

"Probably a couple hundred."

"What type of gun was used in this murder?"

"A 38 Smith and Wesson revolver."

"Did you have an opportunity to examine the gun in this case?"

"Yes."

"Were you also able to lift fingerprints off of the gun?"

Jay Kirschman jumped up and said, "Your honor, we'd like to stipulate that my client's fingerprints were on the barrel of the gun."

Green shot back, "Thank you, Mr. Kirschman, but I'd like to ask my own questions." He turned back to Evans.

"Whose fingerprints were found on the gun?"

"Ron Ramirez."

"Did you match the bullets recovered from the victims' bodies with the gun?"

"Yes. They matched. One Hundred Percent."

"Thank you. I have no further questions."

Judge Jones said, "Your witness, Mr. Kirschman."

"I have no questions at this time, your honor, but I would like to call him back at a later date for further questioning.

Green stood and said he rested his case.

Judge Jones said they would adjourn for the day and defense will begin to present their case in the morning. 9:00 promptly.

As they were leaving the Courthouse, Jay turned to Ricky and Collette and suggested they go out to dinner, relax and go over tomorrow's testimony. Ricky begged off, saying he had something he had to do.

"Ricky, tomorrow's testimony is damned important."

"I know," Ricky answered. "What I have to do is important as well." With that, he walked away, leaving Collette and Jay looking at each other in disbelief.

When he got to his car, he placed a call to Detective Sewell.

"Sewell. Major Case."

"Bill, it's Ricky Burns."

"Hey Ricky. How's your trial going?"

"Can we meet for dinner? I'll buy. I have a favor to ask of you."

"So long as you're buying I'll follow you anywhere."

"Good. Meet me at your deli at 6:00."

"I'll be there."

CHAPTER FORTY-SEVEN

The next morning Ricky got to Martinez' house early. He knocked on the door and the old guy came out dressed, hair slicked down and looking like he was going to church.

"You're looking sharp, Roberto. You're gonna be the hit of the show."

"Is good really?"

"Cops lie. Retired cops don't have a reason to lie. Lucky I'm retired, right? You look great."

"Thank you, sir."

They drove in relative silence with the exception of Ricky reminding him to stick with his story, the truth. Martinez continued to assure him he always tells the truth.

"They're going to try to trick you up, but if you just stick to the truth, you'll be fine."

When they arrived at the Courthouse, Jay, Colette and Bill Barnes were waiting for them in the lobby. Colette was quiet and clearly giving the cold shoulder to Ricky. He called her aside and asked if everything was okay.

"You were in quite a hurry to get out of here last night. I'm sure it was important, but you could've given me a heads up I was going to be alone for the night."

"Collette, when you'll find out where I was, you'll forgive me. I promise, I'll make it up to you if you don't."

"What makes you think I want you to make it up to me?"

"Aw, Collette, give the investigator a break. I'm telling you, it was worth it to miss my company for one little night."

Staring daggers, she told him she'd be the judge of that.

As they walked back to the group, Ricky noticed Martinez heading toward the restroom with a detective right behind him. He thought that couldn't be good and headed toward them as they disappeared into the door.

When he went in, he saw the cop talking to Martinez.

"How many times do you have to be told he doesn't want to talk to you?"

"Let him tell me himself."

"He just did."

Ricky moved between the two of them. The detective reached out to grab Ricky's arm. Ricky turned to him and said, "Don't let your mouth bite off more than your ass can chew."

The detective said, "Fuck you, Burns. When this is over, you're mine!"

Walking away with Martinez, Ricky turned and said, "I'm looking forward to that."

When they got back to the others, Jay noticed Ricky was more agitated than usual. "What happened in there, Ricky?"

"Not important right now. You guys get inside. I'll hang out here with Bill and Roberto 'til you're ready for them."

CHAPTER FORTY-EIGHT

The Defense

Bill Barnes

*I*nside, the courtroom was bedlam. It was packed with people who stood in line for hours hoping to get a seat. Media was there *en masse*, including *Court TV*.

The Bailiff made two attempts to quiet the crowd, then went over to the Judge's bench, grabbed the gavel and banged it several times. Finally, it got quiet and he told everyone to stand for the Honorable Calvin C. Jones.

Once the Judge was seated, he announced that the defense would present its case.

Kirschman stood and called Bill Barnes to the stand. Ricky escorted him into the courtroom. He walked up, was sworn in and sat. Barnes looked sharp. He was wearing an expensive suit and had gotten his hair cut.

"Please state your name."

"William Barnes."

"Mr. Barnes, do you know Ron Ramirez personally?"

"Um, what exactly do you mean by 'personally'? I've met him and talked to him but that's all."

"Let's go back to the night of March 23rd. You went to Club Brick, correct?"

"Yes sir."

"Was the club busy that night?"

"Oh, yes sir. It was packed."

"Were there any scuffles or fights that you witnessed?"

"No sir. It was really busy but there wasn't any trouble."

"Did you see the defendant there?"

"Yes sir."

"So, you met him that night. How did that come about?"

"Well, I saw him there and he's my favorite player on the Demons. So I went over to him and asked if I could take a picture with him."

"And did he do that?"

"At first he said no, but then I told him it was my birthday and how I never miss a game he's playing in. Then he said okay."

"He took a picture with you?"

"Yes. I used my camera and I took a selfie of us."

"What happened after that?"

"He didn't stay long. I saw him leave shortly after our picture."

"About how long would you say he was in the Club before he left?"

"Oh, wow, not more than ten minutes at the most."

"Did you see him again?"

"Yes sir. I followed him out when he was leaving to thank him once more for the picture. The guy he was with got upset that he was talking and he grabbed the keys from Mr. Ramirez and went to get the car."

"Did you go back into the club then?"

"No sir. I stayed and talked to him 'til his friend came back to get him."

"Was there anything unusual that happened?"

"I don't know if you'd call it unusual but when his buddy came back he was in a big hurry. Ron, uh, Mr. Ramirez apologized for having to run. He got in the car right away and his friend screeched out of there."

"So let me get this straight. His friend's driving, pulls up in front of the club, Ron Ramirez jumps in the passenger seat and they speed off. Correct?"

"Yes sir. That's exactly what happened. Then I went back into the Club."

"Did you see Mr. Ramirez with that friend in the Club?"

"No, sir. He was alone, sipping on a drink when I saw him, and then he left."

"Then you followed him out and he was with that friend?"

"Yes, sir."

"Would you describe what his friend looked like to the jury?"

"Um, he was a short Black guy with a nasty attitude."

"Objection," yelled Green.

Judge Jones sustained it and told him not to narrate, just give the physical description.

Barnes looked up at the Judge and apologized.

"I know it's crowded in here but take your time and look around. Do you see Mr. Ramirez' friend in the Courtroom?"

Barnes peered out into the crowd and looked carefully around. After a couple of minutes, he answered, "No, I don't see him."

"You said Ron Ramirez didn't get into any fights or scuffles that night in the Club. How do you know that?"

"I saw him come into Club. I guess I watched him, trying to get up the nerve to ask him to take a birthday picture with me. Then, after we took the picture, he wasn't there much longer. He finished his drink and left after that."

"Did you meet with my investigator, Ricky Burns?"

"Yes, sir."

"Did he show you a group of pictures?"

"Yes, sir, he did."

"Were you able to identify anyone in the pictures?"

"Yes, sir. The friend that was with him that night."

"Thank you, Mr. Barnes. I have no further questions at this time."

Judge Jones looked toward the prosecution table and asked if they had any questions. Both Green and Prentiss shook their heads. The Judge then told Barnes he could step down, which he did quickly and headed out the door.

Roberto Martinez

Jay turned to the jury and announced his next witness to be Roberto Martinez. Again, Ricky appeared with the old man in tow. He pointed to the witness stand and Martinez nodded as he walked up and sat. He was sworn in and the questioning began.

"Please state your name."

"I am Roberto Martinez."

"Mr. Martinez. Are you employed."

"Yes sir Mr. Kirschman."

"Who do you work for?"

"I clean the streets at night for Miami Beach."

"Were you cleaning the streets on Miami Beach the night of March 23rd."

"Si. I mean yes, sir. That's why you told me to come to court."

"Did you see someone shoot anyone that night?"

"Objection, he's leading the witness!"

"Sustained. Rephrase the question, Kirschman."

"Did anything happen that night that was different than most nights."

"Yes sir, Mr. Kirschman."

"Tell the jury what happened that night."

"I saw a car pull up next to another car that was parked. Then this little Black guy got out and shot many times at the people in the car."

"Then what happened?"

"I was so afraid he would see me but he jump back in the car so quickly and in a second he was gone."

"Do you know how many times he shot the people in the car?"

"Not so much. Maybe five or six times. A lot."

"Do you think you could recognize him again?"

"Si, si! I was so scared, I will never forget that face!"

"I know it's crowded in here, but I'd like you to look carefully around the courtroom and see if you see that man in here."

The old man's eyes got big as he stared, open mouthed at Jay.

"It's okay. Nothing can happen to you if you see him. You're safe here in the Courtroom."

With that, Martinez slowly eyed the entire crowd. "No, sir, Mr. Kirschman. I don't see him anywhere here."

"You're sure of that?"

"Si. Yes, sir, Mr. Kirschman."

"Did you meet with my investigator, Ricky Burns?"

"Oh yes. He is a very nice man."

"Yes, he is. He's also very good at what he does. Did he show you pictures when you met with him?"

"He show me pictures of many men."

"Did you recognize any of the men in the pictures?"

"Si. Yes. The little Black man's picture was in there."

"Did you report the shooting to the police?"

"No, sir. I want to forget I saw it, but I can't. His face comes in the night when I am trying to sleep. I am always looking around when I am cleaning at night that he is not watching me. I no want to be involved."

"How did you get involved then?"

"Mr. Ricky. He came to me one morning soon before I was going to go home. He asks me about that night and if maybe I saw something happen."

I don't tell no lies. I tell him what I saw. Then we go to have some breakfast and he shows me so many pictures. And there he was. I see the man who shot those people."

"Thank you Mr. Martinez. That's all for now."

Judge Jones asked if the prosecution had any questions and Prentis, looking somewhat confused, said, "Not at this time."

"Okay, Mr. Kirschman. Your next witness?"

Prentiss stood and said, "Your Honor, could we possibly take a break for a short while?"

Jones responded, "Tell you what. It's getting late. Let's adjourn for the day and begin again tomorrow morning at 9:00 promptly."

CHAPTER FORTY-NINE

As they left the Courthouse, Jay suggested they go back to the office to discuss Ricky's testimony tomorrow. He was going to testify to the photo array and explain how Martinez identified JoJo. Collette asked about dinner. Jay wanted to order in from the restaurant downstairs in his building.

"It'll save time and we won't have to keep our voices so low that we can't hear each other, much less the chatter around us."

They all agreed. When they got to the office, Collette called and ordered Reubens and fries for them. Not five minutes after they sat down, Ricky's phone buzzed. He looked at it and said, "I've got to take this. It's important. I'll be back in a minute."

Collette piped up, "You skipping out on dinner with us again, Mr. Burns?"

Ricky smiled at her and shook his head.

Once he was alone, Ricky answered, "Bill, what's up?"

"We got the ballistics back. You called it. The bullets matched both scenes. If it's Jackson's gun, you've got yourself a case."

"I knew it. I had a feeling all along. Thanks, I owe you one."

"Yes, you do. Keep that in mind," Sewell laughed.

"So are you going to arrest him for it?"

"Not now."

"What do you mean 'not now'? You've got him dead to rights, and my guy is being tried for the murders. That just ain't right!"

"It's not me, man. It's coming from the top. No arrest until Ramirez' trial is over."

"Sonovabitch! That's as cold as it gets."

"Sorry. I did try, but my hands are tied now."

After a short silence, Ricky ended the call and headed back in to tell Jay and Collette the good news.

Ricky walked back into Jay's inner sanctum and said, "Your Florida cops are the worst!"

"What happened," Jay and Collette asked in unison.

"That was Sewell. I'd asked him to get to Evans, their ballistics guy, to compare the gun to Jackson's shooting up the building and the guy that was shot in the night club."

"And?" Jay interrupted.

"They match."

"So we're home free. When are they arresting the little one-eyed creep, or have they already?"

"I'm so freaking mad about this!"

"You're a funny guy, Ricky. I've never heard you curse and I know you're really pissed. Can't you even curse when you're this mad?" Jay smiled and Collette laughed.

"No freaking way. Been there done that. I cleaned up my act after I left Major Crimes. I have no plans to backtrack. I'm plenty angry, though. They're refusing to arrest him until the Ramirez trial is over."

"That's them. All they want is a conviction, and they don't give a flying fuck about whether it's the right guy."

"Well, they're not getting a conviction this time. Let's get to work."

The meeting lasted about three hours. Ricky was ready to hit the stand and do some damage to the State's case.

"I'm not even going to ask if you need a ride, Collette," Jay said.

"You're smarter than the average attorney, boss," Collette smiled and looked toward Ricky.

Ricky nodded. As they left the office, Jay said, "I thought so."

CHAPTER FIFTY

Ricky Burns

The trial started at precisely 9:00 the next morning. Jay called Ricky to the stand. After he was sworn in, Jay asked, "What's your background in law enforcement?"

"I recently retired as a First Grade detective from the Police Department in New York City. My last command was the Major Crimes Unit."

"As a detective in the Major Crimes Unit did you ever work homicides?"

"Yes, mostly homicides."

"When you were working Major Crimes, did you receive any awards or citations?"

"Yes, I received numerous awards, including the Combat Cross."

"What exactly is a Combat Cross?"

"It's the second highest medal you can get, given only to police who have been in shoot-outs."

"What do you do now that you've retired?"

"I'm a licensed Private Investigator in the State of Florida."

"Were you retained by me as a Private Investigator to assist in the Ron Ramirez case?"

"Yes, I was."

"During your investigation did you speak with William Barnes?"

"Yes."

"What did you discuss with him?"

"We talked about the night of March 23rd, and what happened at Club Brick that night."

"Did you have an opportunity to show Mr. Barnes any photographs?"

"Yes, I made a photo array of six pictures, one of which was JoJo Jackson."

Jay walked back to the defense table and picked up a stack of photos. Walking back to the witness stand, he handed the pictures to Ricky.

"Is this the group of photos you showed Mr. Barnes?"

Ricky shuffled through the photos and looking up at Jay said, "Yes, it is."

"Did he identify anyone in those pictures?"

"Yes. He pointed out JoJo Jackson and said he was the friend that was with Ramirez that night."

"Did you also have the opportunity to speak with Roberto Martinez?"

"Yes, I did."

"How did you and Mr. Martinez meet?"

"I canvassed the area of the murders at about the time the murders took place and saw Mr. Martinez cleaning the streets. I introduced myself and during our conversation he told me he had witnessed the murders."

Green jumped to his feet, "Objection! Hearsay."

"Overruled. I'll allow it."

"Did you show Mr. Martinez any pictures?"

"Yes. I made a photo array of six pictures. JoJo Jackson was one of them. Mr. Martinez picked out Jackson and said he was the one he saw shoot the men in the car."

At that moment the Courtroom exploded. Photographers were snapping pictures, media representatives ran out the door to announce breaking news, and it seemed as though every spectator was talking.

Prentiss was shouting "Objection! Objection!"

Judge Jones slammed his gavel several times. As the crowd noise began to subside, he yelled, "Quiet!

Quiet in this Courtroom! I'll throw everyone out if this happens again," and it was suddenly silent.

"What is your objection, Ms. Prentiss?"

"Hearsay, your Honor."

"Sustained." Looking toward the jury, he advised them to disregard Burns' answer.

"I have no further questions."

Jones asked if the prosecution wanted to cross. Green stood, looking disgustedly at Burns, and said "We have no questions."

The Judge told Ricky to take his seat, then said, "Your next witness, Mr. Kirschman?"

Ricky was visibly upset. As he passed Jay, he whispered "The freaking Judge is trying to save the prosecution!"

Jay smiled and whispered back, "That's not a problem. The jury can't unhear what they've already heard."

At that point Kirschman called Detective Cameron Evans to the stand.

Green leaned over to Prentiss and whispered, "What the fuck is this about?"

Prentiss' homely face was blank. "I don't know. Kirschman always has something up his sleeve."

Green added, "I'm not crazy about his new investigator, either. I'll bet that fucker had something to do with whatever is coming. With Burns on his side, he's even worse!"

Detective Cameron Evans

Evans takes the stand and Judge Jones reminds him he is still under oath. Evans nodded and said, "Yes, Your Honor, I've done this before."

"Detective Evans, prior to this case have you ever found fingerprints on the barrel of a gun and nowhere else, including the handle and trigger?"

"I don't know. I've examined hundreds of guns."

"Then would you agree with me that it's unusual to find fingerprints only on the barrel and nowhere else on the gun?"

Evans begrudgingly agreed.

"Okay. We agree on that so let's get to a couple of other things we may agree on. Did you have a chance to compare the bullets recovered from a shooting at 4256 S.W. 33 Avenue in Liberty City and the gun in this case?"

"Yes, I did."

"And what did you learn? Was it a match?"

"Yes, the bullets recovered from the apartment building came from the gun used in the shooting in this case."

"Did you also have an opportunity to compare the bullet recovered from the victim of a shooting at Club Z?"

"Yes."

"Did it match?"

"Yes."

"So let's get this straight. We can agree the gun used to shoot up the apartment building in Liberty City was used to shoot the victim at Club Z and the victims in his case."

"Yes."

"Can we also agree that fingerprints only on the barrel could be consistent with someone wearing gloves holding its handle handing it to someone who had no gloves?"

Green jumped up and yelled, "Objection! Calls for speculation."

Judge Jones said, "Good try, counselor, but I'm going to allow him to answer this one."

Evans said it would be consistent.

"No further questions, Your Honor," Jay said, walking back to the defense table and winking at Collette.

Judge Jones asked if the prosecution had any further questions. Green mumbled, "No, Your Honor."

At this point, Kirschman asked for a sidebar and the Judge motioned to the prosecutors to come to the bench.

"Your Honor," Kirschman said, "Based on the evidence presented, I'd like to move for a directed verdict of Not Guilty."

"That'll have to be done in open Court." The Judge looked to the Jury and told them they were dismissed for the day. They stood immediately and quickly left the Courtroom. It looked as though they wanted to get out before the Judge changed his mind.

Once the Jury was out of the room, Kirschman moved for a directed verdict of Not Guilty on the basis of eyewitness testimony and ballistics. The Judge smiled. "I'm going to have to deny that motion, Mr. Kirschman. I think we're going to leave this for the Jury to decide."

As Jay, Collette and Ricky were leaving, Jay told Collette to call Ramirez and get him into the office so they could prepare him to testify tomorrow.

"Boss, are you sure you want to put him on the stand?"

"No, but let's prep him then make a definitive decision."

"He's such a hot head," she replied.

"I think it's a good idea, if we can tame him enough, but either way it's a gamble," Ricky added.

"That's for damn sure," Jay said, "But we've got to try."

CHAPTER FIFTY-ONE

*W*hen they arrived at the office, Ramirez was standing outside the office door waiting. Collette told him to come in as Jay unlocked the door. They went straight to Jay's private office and sat.

"Why am I here this time?" Ron asked.

"We need to decide whether or not to put you on the stand," Jay answered.

"I told you I want to testify. It's *my* life, man!"

Ricky spoke up. "Well, we want to get a not guilty verdict, and in my opinion, we've got this case won now. You testify and make one wrong move, you're going to blow the whole thing."

Jay agreed. Collette sat there nodding her head.

"I want to tell my side of the story. I want to bury that little one-eyed bastard."

Ricky shook his head in frustration. "He'll be locked up as soon as the trial is over without your testimony."

"Listen to him, Ron. He's not wrong. We're in a good place right now," Jay told him.

Ramirez pouted but didn't speak.

After a couple of minutes of strained silence, Jay said, "Well, let's get you prepped. Let's start by telling us about the night of the murders."

Ramirez went through the evening detail by detail, looking good. When he finished, Jay told him so, and said, "Now we're going to play prosecutors. They're going to say and do everything they can to get you to break, so hold tight."

"Don't worry about me. I won't snap. Just ask the questions. I'm gonna need to get some sleep tonight."

"Mr. Ramirez, you picked Mr. Jackson up and drove to the club with him that night, correct?"

"Yes."

"And you've picked him up and gone to clubs with him on numerous occasions in the past?"

"Yeah, that's right."

Jay grinned. "Okay, Mr. Ramirez, why would a man who's been your close friend and lover for years turn on you?"

Ramirez practically jumped out of his chair. "Fuck you! I told you it was one lousy blow job!"

"That's exactly why we don't want to put you on the stand. The romance angle is going to be brought up. Count on it. They'll also bring in those texts between you two. How many times did you say you loved each other in them?" Ricky asked.

Ron sat back down. "Okay. I get it now. Really. I've got this. No more outbursts. You don't have to worry about me."

Ricky grimaced. "Oh, we won't worry. If you screw this up, you're the one going to jail, not us."

Jay then asked again, "Why would a man who's been your close friend and lover for years turn on you?"

"One quick blow job does not make us life-long lovers," Ramirez calmly answered.

Ricky nodded and told him not to use the term 'blow job' in Court. "Try 'encounters.' Remember, you're playing to the jury."

"We found some texts between you and Mr. Jackson. How many times would you estimate you two used the word 'love' in those texts?"

Ron swallowed and took a breath. "He was trying to blackmail me for money. That's all the texts were about."

"Perfect," Jay said.

The questioning went on for more than an hour without Ron losing his temper again. Ramirez went home for his night's sleep. Jay and Ricky agreed that he'd done well after the blow-up.

"Let's just hope he can hold it together tomorrow," Collette said.

Ricky frowned. "I feel better but who knows what Green and Prentiss have planned to break him."

"Whatever," Collette said. "You both warned him. Now it's on him."

"I just hate to lose. Especially when my client is innocent," Jay added.

After a short discussion about plans for the next morning, they all got up to leave. Jay looked at Collette and said, "I suppose you've got a ride."

Collette and Ricky nodded in unison and Jay laughed, "I knew it!"

On the drive home, Ricky told Collette there was a great little bar at the Marina, and maybe they should stop and have a nightcap.

"I'd really love to, Ricky, but it's such a long drive to my place from there, and we have an early morning call."

"Don't worry about the drive, I don't plan on taking you anywhere near your place tonight."

"Oh my," Collette feigned surprise. "If that's the way you feel, who am I to fight it?"'

CHAPTER FIFTY-TWO

The next morning at 8:00, Jay, Ricky and Collette arrived at the Courthouse. They first looked for Ramirez who was nowhere to be found.

Jay looked at Ricky and asked if he thought Ron was ready for what was coming today.

"Jay, I don't really like the guy. We advised him not to testify and he insisted. We know he's already killed one guy, and there's not a doubt in my mind that he shot JoJo in his head. If he screws up, it's on him, not us. The important thing is to get justice. If he goes to jail by his own testimony, justice will be served."

"Yeah...but I hate to lose. Especially when he really is innocent in this particular case."

"I'm just saying, the guy is doing it to himself. I'm not the sharpest spoon in the drawer, but if my attorney told me not to get on the stand, especially because he felt he had the case won, I'd be paying attention."

"It is what it is and we'll just have to deal with it."

"What if he skipped out?" Collette asked.

Jay laughed. "Well, we got paid up front so if he runs, he runs."

Ricky smiled. "Now you're talking."

Just then they saw Ramirez walk through the door. Collette waved him over to where they were sitting.

"You're looking tired, Ron. Is everything okay?" Jay asked.

"I'm feeling a little nervous about all this. I didn't sleep well."

Jay looked at Ramirez until the football player was looking back at him and he knew he had his full attention.

"Ron, you don't have to do this. We've presented a great case. Every lie or omission from them, we managed to refute and cancel. I could see it in the jury's eyes. The possibility of you making one wrong move and losing the jury is big."

"I hear you, Mr. Kirschman. I just want them to hear the truth from me. I know I can handle it now. Besides, I want that little one-eyed motherfucker to go down."

"I understand, but again, I have to advise against it."

"I don't care. I need to face them and let them see who I am."

"Don't show them too much of who you are, kid. That could blow the whole thing," Ricky said.

"You I can live without, man. You been against me from the beginning!"

Jay raised his voice, "Hey, that's enough. Ricky's the one who found all the evidence to save your sorry ass. Show some respect."

Ron lowered his head and mumbled "Sorry, man. I guess I'm more nervous than I thought."

"Whatever," Jay said. "Don't bite the hand that feeds you."

CHAPTER FIFTY-THREE

They seated themselves at their table in the Courtroom and made small talk as the room filled. The line for seats started early. Everyone wanted to see Ron Ramirez testify.

"I guess it didn't matter that they're televising this. Look at this crowd," Collette said.

"Only the lazy fans are staying home to watch it on television," Jay quipped. "I wish they'd get on with this. It's after nine now."

"You didn't expect this circus to start promptly, did you?" Ricky asked.

"It has every other day," Ron injected.

"I guess the word is out that you're testifying." Jay looked around again and nodded. "Yeah, there's the Bailiff. Good. Get ready, Ron."

Just as Jay said that the Bailiff came over to them.

"Is this guy a lawyer?" he asked, pointing to Ricky.

"No," Jay responded, "Mr. Burns is my investigator."

"Sorry, chum, only lawyers and legal assistants up here. You can sit in the first row, but you ain't sitting there."

Ricky got up immediately, looked at the Bailiff and said, "Yeah, I'm fond of you, too." Then he squeezed his way into the first row.

` After the Court was called to order and the crowd had calmed and was quiet, Jay called Ron Ramirez to the stand.

After Ron was sworn in and seated, Jay stood before him and asked his name.

"Ronald Ramirez."

"And how old are you Mr. Ramirez?"

"Twenty-four."

"Are you employed?"

"I'm pretty sure I am."

"Pretty sure?"

"Well, I can't do much until this trial is over."

"Okay. What do you do when you're working?"

"I'm a wide receiver."

"For what team?"

"The Miami Demons."

"Have you ever been arrested?"

"Yes sir. When I was in high school and college. I got into fights."

"Have you ever served time for any of those incidents?"

"No sir. I did community service and paid fines."

"Did you recently sign a forty million dollar contract for your services?"

"Yes, I did."

"And did you receive twenty-four million guaranteed and up front?"

"Yes sir, I did.

"So you really have no reason to kill anyone for drugs, do you?"

"Objection!" Green shouted. "Speculation."

"I withdraw the question." Kirschman tried hard to not look smug.

"Do you know JoJo Jackson?"

"I do."

"How long have you known him?"

"I've known him since middle school. He's too small to play but loves football. So after I got my contract I asked him if he wanted to be my assistant."

"What does being your assistant entail?"

"He carries my bag, keeps me hydrated on the field, and does most of my driving for me."

"Do you smoke marijuana?"

"Yes. Most of us football players do. It helps with the pain."

"Where do you get your marijuana from?"

"JoJo Jackson. He sells drugs. That's how he makes his living."

"Have you ever witnessed Mr. Jackson selling to someone other than you?"

"Yes. Lots of times."

"Let's go back to the night of the murders. How long were you in Club Brick that night?'

"I guess, maybe ten minutes, if that. I got a drink but the place was packed and there were no VIP Rooms available."

"Did anything happen while you were in the club? Did you get into any scuffles?"

"No. The place was so crowded. I took a picture with some guy for his birthday. Then I was afraid everyone would want pictures and autographs. I didn't even finish the one drink I ordered and I left."

"Was your car valeted?

"No. I don't like strangers driving my car. We parked in a lot a coupla blocks away."

"So what happened when you stepped outside the Club?"

"The guy who I took a picture with came out to thank me again. JoJo had an attitude about something and didn't want to wait 'til I finished talking. So he took my keys and went to get the car."

"Did anything unusual happen?"

"How do you mean 'unusual'?"

"Out of the ordinary."

"Well, when JoJo picked me up, he was driving crazy. When we got away from the club, I saw his gun on the console and asked him what that was about. He told me he had a problem with one of his drug deals so he took care of some business. Then he handed it to me and told me to toss it when we got to a certain place."

"Did you do that?"

"Yes."

"How did you handle the gun?"

"I held it by the barrel."

"Was JoJo wearing gloves?"

"Yes. Most of the time when he's driving, he wears gloves."

"Then where did you go?"

"We went to Prime 112 but it was closed. So JoJo said we should go to his girl's house and she'd feed us."

"So you ate at her house?"

"No."

"Why not?"

"I used her computer to try to see if whatever JoJo had gotten into was already on the web."

"Was it?"

"No, and I had a bad feeling about things."

"Where was JoJo while you were on the computer?"

"He was in the other room making out with his girl."

"So what did you do?"

"I took off. Went home and went to bed."

"Did you see Mr. Jackson after that night?"

"No. When I saw the shootings on the news the next morning, I realized that hanging out with him was bad for my career. I didn't call him. He must have figured it out because he didn't call me either. I didn't hear from him again until I got charged with these murders."

"He called you after you were charged?"

"No. He started sending me weird texts. He was trying to blackmail me."

"What would he blackmail you for?"

"He was trying to shake me down for money. He'd threatened to say I killed those guys if I didn't pay him."

"Did you pay him?"

"No. I didn't pay him because I didn't murder those two guys."

"When you were arrested, did you tell the police officers you didn't do it?

"Yes, of course."

"Did you tell them anything else?"

"No. I learned a long time ago you don't talk to cops."

"Thank you, Mr. Ramirez. I have no further questions."

The Judge looked over at the prosecution table and told the attorneys Ramirez was their witness.

Green got up and didn't waste any time going after Ramirez.

"You know not to speak to the police? Honest people talk to the police."

"I was being honest when I told them I didn't do it, but I've seen how they can twist your words so that was all I said besides, 'I want to call my attorney.' They didn't come to talk to me. They came to arrest me."

"Okay. The night of the murders. You drove to the club and he drove back?"

"Yes, that's right."

"If Mr. Jackson did most of your driving, why did you pick him up that night?"

"I was already driving so I didn't see any reason to play diva and refuse to drive. Besides, he drives most of the time for me, but not all the time."

"In the past, you mentioned you'd been arrested for fighting. How many times?"

"Several times, but there's a reason. I'm a football player and when I'm out and people have been drinking, they get beer muscles and want to try me. Most times it doesn't work out so well for them."

"Did you and Mr. Jackson have any interaction after you were arrested?"

"Only through texts."

"About those texts. You two mentioned love a lot in them. Is it true you had been having a sexual relationship with him."

"No."

"Remember Mr. Ramirez, you are under oath."

"I know I am. We didn't have a sexual relationship. One time doesn't make a relationship." Then, voice rising, "I'll bet you've had one-timers, too, that didn't end in a relationship."

The Judge glared at Ron and said, "Just answer the questions, Mr. Ramirez."

Green continued. "So the night of the murders, you saw the gun on your console. Do you always keep a gun in your car?"

"No. It wasn't my gun."

"So he drove you to his girlfriend's house to get something to eat, but you got on her computer instead. You were trying to find out if a shooting was reported that night. You knew there was a shooting because you were there. Is that correct?"

"No. I figured there'd been a shooting because he asked me to throw his gun out the window."

"Let's go back to your one-night stand. Are you sure it wasn't a prolonged love affair that Mr. Jackson broke off?

"I'm sure."

"Maybe you're a scorned lover?"

"No. I experimented once. I have a fiancé. She's a female and we have a son."

"A lot of people are married with children, but on the side..."

Ramirez interrupted. "I'm not one of them."

"Isn't that why you shot him?"

"I didn't shoot him!" Ramirez' voice was rising.

"Didn't you try to kill him?"

"If I tried to kill him, he'd be dead!" he practically shouted.

Jay turned to Ricky. "Oh, oh, here we go."

"I'm holding my breath, Jay."

Green, pleased with himself for finally getting Ramirez' riled, said "Just like those two other guys are dead now, huh?"

Ramirez jumped up "I didn't kill them!"

And Kirschman stood and shouted, "Objection!"

Green calmly turned away from Ramirez and said, "I have no further questions."

Still standing from his objection, Jay asked to redirect and Judge Jones told him to go ahead. He walked over to his client and asked, "Did you get into a scuffle that night at the club?"

"No, I did not."

"Did you kill those two young men?"

"No sir, I did not."

"No further questions."

Judge Jones looked up at the clock and said, "We'll adjourn for the day and closing arguments will start at 9:00 sharp tomorrow morning."

As Jay, Collette, Ricky and Ron walked out of the Courthouse, they were mobbed by the media whores.

"Ron! Ron! Give us a statement?"

Jay looked at the crowd and spoke. "Mr. Ramirez will not be giving any statements at this time. Please direct any questions to me.

One of the reporters shouted, "Okay, Mr. Kirschman, how's the case going?"

"I feel quite confident about the case. My client is innocent and we are proving it. That's all I have to say for now, but after the verdict, regardless of the outcome, I will tell you everything."

Ricky stepped in and told the reporters it was over, and Jay, Collette. Ron and Ricky walked away.

CHAPTER FIFTY-FOUR

The next morning the Courthouse was mobbed. The defense team tried to push through the crowds but were recognized. Everyone was yelling questions and trying to touch the football player.

Ricky looked at Jay and said, "You and Colette go in through the attorneys' entrance. I'll stay with Ron and be sure he gets into the Courtroom without being mauled or answering questions."

"Great idea, big guy," Collette winked, and Ricky went weak in the knees.

As soon as he recovered his composure, he put an arm around Ramirez and hustled him through the crowd.

It took several minutes for the Bailiff to quiet the crowd. When it finally was calm enough, he told everyone to rise for The Honorable Calvin J. Jones. Once the Judge was seated, he spoke to the Jury.

"Today we begin the closing arguments. The attorneys will give a summation of their case. Be aware, it is not evidence. It is strictly to give you an overview of what they have presented throughout the trial. The prosecution will go first. Mr. Green, Ms. Prentiss?"

Green walked up to the Jury and began.

"Ladies and Gentlemen of the Jury, I want to thank you for your attention and patience throughout the presentation of this case. I won't take up much of your time because this is an open and shut case.

"We've had a witness tell us about a scuffle in Club Brick the night of the murder. We also learned Ramirez searched a computer to see if the murders had made the news that same night.

"A ballistics expert from the Miami Beach Police Department testified that the only prints on the gun used in these murders belonged to the defendant.

"You've heard from the defense that there were other crimes committed with the same gun. That has nothing to do with the case at hand. Your only responsibility is to consider the facts of this case. No other issues can be considered.

"You've also seen text messages between Mr. Jackson and the defendant. 'Love' is mentioned in those texts. So you've seen just how close they were. Only someone that close would recognize who the defendant really is and what he did.

"To sum it up, we have a scuffle at the nightclub, a double murder, and a murder weapon with the defendant's prints on it. There is only one correct verdict in this case. I ask that you find the defendant guilty of two counts of murder and one count of attempted murder.

"Again, thank you for your time and patience."

With that, Green went back to the prosecution table. Judge Jones told Kirschman the floor was his.

Jay stood. As he walked toward the Jury, he began speaking.

"Ladies and gentlemen, I wish I could tell you this isn't going to take up much of your time, but I actually have something to say. Let's walk through the case together.

"The only person who told you about a scuffle in the club was JoJo Jackson. We will be getting to him a little later.

"You heard from a witness that Mr. Ramirez was not in any scuffle that night but instead, cordially took a picture with him. Being a fan, he watched Mr. Ramirez from the moment he walked in the club that night. He testified under oath that the football player was only in the club for ten minutes at the most."

Looking toward the minority jurors, he continued. "The police didn't care about these murders, and they made a joke of the crime scene. The procedures they carried out were sloppy at best. To them it was just another couple of Black guys dealing drugs. They contaminated the crime scene then moved it because they were more concerned with snarling up morning traffic than they were about those poor, dead Black men. They didn't even care enough to canvass the area for anyone who might have witnessed the shooting. Canvassing, or looking for witnesses, is normal procedure in any homicide. They didn't care enough to even do that.

"But we did. We canvassed the area and found an eyewitness to the shooting. What did the eyewitness tell us? He said it was a short Black man that he saw shoot into that car. Mr. Ramirez is six-foot four and couldn't possibly be confused for a short man. The same witness identified JoJo Jackson as the person he saw shoot into the car, killing those two young Black men and wounding a third.

"Let's talk about JoJo Jackson for a minute. JoJo Jackson admitted he was getting a sweet deal from the prosecutors for shooting another person in a different night club. The prosecutors' own Ballistics Expert testified that the same gun was used in two other shootings; one in a nightclub where he seriously injured someone and another to shoot up an apartment building.

"You heard JoJo Jackson testify that the gun that was used in this double murder, the gun that was used at an apartment shooting and another nightclub shooting was his.

"When you consider all this evidence, there is *more* than reasonable doubt here and I ask that you find the defendant, Ron Ramirez, not guilty. Thank you for your patience."

Judge Jones then turned to the Jury. "Ladies and Gentlemen, the case now goes to you. You're to follow the instructions I'm about to give you. You will be taken to the deliberation room. The Bailiff will confiscate all of your cell phones. You are to have no communication with anyone other than the other jurors. If you have a question about anything, the Bailiff will be right outside your door. Write it down and he will deliver it to me. We will get you the answer."

With that, the Bailiff took the jurors to begin their deliberation.

Once the Jury was out of ear shot, the Judge advised the attorneys to stay close. "You'll be notified if there are any questions and when the verdict is returned."

CHAPTER FIFTY-FIVE

Jay had reserved a private room in a restaurant close to the Courthouse so they wouldn't be bothered by onlookers. Ramirez was silent but the other three had a lot to talk about.

"Hey boss. This was a great idea. We're not used to having our client with us while we wait for a verdict. Do I have a price limit or can I order whatever I want? I love Italian food."

"Go for it. I don't think there's anything on the menu that will break me."

"Thanks. I'm going to have the veal."

After the food was served, they were quiet for a few minutes but then the conversation got lively and even Ramirez lightened up and started talking.

"I hope you're right about the verdict, Jay. I want to get back to playing ball. The Demons just signed a new quarterback. He's good and I think the team will have a great season. I'm thinking that the worst we can do is win the Division. I can't wait to get back on the field and sweat again."

Jay smiled at the player. "I can't make any promises but I feel really good about this, Ron. They didn't have shit. They should have arrested JoJo and dismissed the charges against you when the Ballistics guy connected the gun to all three crime scenes. Hard heads. They could have made themselves look good but a not guilty verdict isn't going to do that."

The conversation got lively, almost as if they'd forgotten why they were there. Ron regaled them with football anecdotes from his playing years. He told some stories about when he was younger that had the whole group laughing out loud.

They were seeing a side of Ramirez they'd not seen before, and even Ricky was beginning to like him. It was a cordial afternoon.

Ramirez was on his third cannoli when Jay's phone rang. Collette stopped in the middle of a word and they all went silent as they watched Jay nod and say they would be there.

"It was the Bailiff. The verdict is in and he wants us back in the Courtroom in thirty minutes."

Ron Ramirez, for the first time, looked scared. It had finally dawned on him that twelve complete strangers were going to decide whether or not he'd ever play football again. Very quietly, he said, "It's only been a coupla hours. Awful fast. Is that bad?

Jay told him it was a good sign. "When they come back this quickly it's usually favorable. Take it easy. We'll know soon enough." Then he motioned the waiter for the bill, paid it and they headed back to hear the verdict.

CHAPTER FIFTY-SIX

The Courtroom was a chaotic scene. It was packed. Judge Jones was banging his gavel and the Bailiff was shouting for quiet. The Judge admonished the crowd that when the verdict was read, he expected quiet.

"I know some of you have strong emotions one way or the other but save your outbursts for when you leave. I won't tolerate any yelling, and if you have to cry, cry quietly. This is a murder trial and I expect respect to be shown."

Ricky looked around and made a mental note of the fact that JoJo was nowhere to be seen. He wondered if he had gotten out of Dodge while the getting was good.

The Bailiff brought the Jury in and they took their seats. They were a somber looking group. Not one of them glanced at the defense table.

Jay leaned close to Collette and whispered, "I don't like the looks of this."

The Judge looked at the Jury and asked if they had reached a verdict. The foreperson told him they had. The Bailiff went over and took a piece of paper from her and handed it to the Judge. After he looked at the verdict, he handed it to the Bailiff who took it to the Clerk. Judge

Jones asked that she read it to the Court. Jay and Ron stood as the verdict was read.

"Count I of Murder in the First Degree. Not guilty. Count II of Murder in the First Degree, Not Guilty. Count III Attempted Murder, Not Guilty."

Jay grabbed Ramirez' arm because he had started to go limp. "It's okay. It's over, Ron. You're a free man." Ron straightened up and tears ran down his cheeks. He turned to Jay and the two hugged. Then he turned to Ricky who was in the first row now standing. They hugged, and Ron spoke softly into his ear. "I know you're still a cop at heart but the murder I told you about stays with us, right?"

Ricky smiled. "I know the rules. Your secret is safe with me." And then he thought to himself, "It'll catch up with him eventually."

CHAPTER FIFTY-SEVEN

When they got outside, Green and Prentiss were already at the microphone. Green told the reporters he wasn't happy with the verdict, "but that's our criminal justice system and I respect it."

The media was shouting questions but they waved them off and turned to leave. Green shook Jay's hand and said, "Good work." Then Jay, Ricky, Ron and Collette stepped up to the mikes.

"What about JoJo Jackson?"

"We expect that JoJo Jackson will be arrested and charged for the murders soon."

"Was it just dumb luck that you found the witnesses?"

"Absolutely not. My investigator is a seasoned detective," and he looked toward Ricky, "Just did what the cops should have done the night of the murders or in any homicide investigation."

Suddenly, the crowd started backing away and some people were even running. Ricky turned to see what had spooked them. Standing behind them was JoJo Jackson with a gun. Instinctively he grabbed Collette and pushed her down to the ground and laid on her for protection. He heard a shot. Ramirez fell next to him bleeding profusely from his head. He looked up. JoJo was moving toward Ron. Before Ricky could do anything to stop him, JoJo fired another shot into the football player's head. Standing over him, smiling broadly, JoJo said, "Didn't you see the movie, asshole, it's two in the head."

ABOUT THE AUTHORS

C. K. Laurence is known for her unusual desire to do "one of everything" before she leaves this world. She's close to her goal. She's been a legal assistant, a high school teacher, a director's assistant in movies and commercials, had a radio show, created Claudia's Kitchen (which she says had the best cookies, cakes and pies ever baked), worked in politics on Gubernatorial, House, Senate and Presidential campaigns (including driving in motorcades) and finally, an author.

Jerry Lyons is a retired First Grade Detective from New York City where he worked in the Major Case Unit investigating murder and rape cases. He received numerous medals, including the Combat Cross, one of the highest awards given. Because of his love for investigations, after leaving the police force he became a Private Investigator. For the past fifteen years he's been involved on the winning side of some of the most high profile cases in the country such as Casey Anthony, Aaron Hernandez (former Patriot Tight End) and Gary Giordano. He's always on the winning side.

Made in the USA
Columbia, SC
28 September 2024

43257976R00124